I had walked across the Common from the Hall of Music, open-throated to the spring, rejoicing in a wave of yellow crocus awakened from their bed of snow, dreaming of lilacs when I saw her standing alone, aslant from her own shadow as it shortened toward noon. She was hatless and golden in the sun, wearing the traditional red and black check mackinaw of college students and North Shore fishermen. The usual short boots, the usual wool trousers, the usual books under her arm. What was unusual was the directness of her gaze and the invitation in her stance.

She gazed at me for one more confident moment, shifted her books from one hip to the other and said with an admirable simplicity and calm, "You've been watching me for days. It's time to know why."

A *Certain* Discontent

CLEVE BOUTELL

The Naiad Press, Inc.
1992

Printed in the United States of America on acid-free paper
First Edition

Edited by Katherine V. Forrest
Cover design by Pat Tong and Bonnie Liss
    (Phoenix Graphics)
Typeset by Sandi Stancil

Library of Congress Cataloging-in-Publication Data

Boutell, Cleve.
    A certain discontent / by Cleve Boutell.
        p.   cm.
    ISBN 1-56280-009-4
    I. Title.
PS3552.0836C4   1992
813′.54--dc20
                                                    91-37469
                                                        CIP

For Bo

About the Author

A successful twenty-year career as a publications art director concluded, Cleve says "For fun and enlightenment I collect rare books, am an amateur student of Russian history, do my three miles every other day, read omnivorously, and live in Pasadena, California with two patient alley cats." She has previously published short fiction, and is currently a contributing editor of Small Press Magazine. *A Certain Discontent* is her first novel.

A Certain Discontent

Last week, I appeared with my grandniece at the inquest into her father's death. The determination: accidental death by shooting. Fritz Becker stumbled and fell while attempting to move a duck boat into open water, discharging the gun he carried. Joanna testified that the gun, a double-barreled Italian Bernardelli shotgun, which her father had originally given to her the year before, was a sensitive, responsive gun and she believed that he had never known how to handle it.

Choosing not to remain a ward of the court until she reached her majority, Joanna settled the matter. I am the only living relative whose existence she concedes, let alone to whom she would surrender control over herself for however brief a period.

I find no great tragedy in Fritz Becker's death; only in his life and the result of it on his wife Maria. Because Joanna often found that life to her liking, or that it was simply wise and necessary to take an active part in her father's interests, to acquiesce in his pleasures, suggests only that she had learned to perfection the selective art of withholding herself. That she was in any real sense being shaped by him was a delusion only he held, and a fear held by her mother as long as Maria had lived.

At the end of the day the inquest closed, Joanna drove me back to the house on the river bluff through a winter dusk closing down in silence behind us. Crossing the bridge, I watched the river flowing dull, opaque and gray, each lamp along the bridge a cold, contracted glow. Whatever Joanna's thoughts may have been, they were kept in the chill sanctuary of that same silence until I remarked that I was glad it was all over, and she looked at me with a thin smile and replied that she hadn't noticed. It had been over for a long time.

It has been two years since the night Fritz Becker telephoned asking me to come to Minneapolis. His wife was dying. He was uneasy about Joanna, he could no longer deal with the situation. And it was clear that he no longer wanted to.

I suppose I will always remember that my train arrived from Duluth forty minutes late in a driving rain; that the last hour the pace was cautious, halting, and aggravated by unscheduled stops; a mockery of my concerns. Rain streamed down the windows of my compartment. Red warning lights hung in shimmering crosses along the tracks, and a trail of yellow lanterns swam in the impenetrable dark. As the train slowly crossed the river and came into the city, I locked my three bags and put them outside the door of my compartment for the porter. I put my coat, my umbrella, and the book I had been reading, on the seat beside me. Abruptly, the rain stopped.

The train had entered the yards and moved like a sword into the scabbard of its green shed scattering its own light on a crush of baggage trucks and porters and people craning necks, scanning windows for a glimpse of familiar face or figure. I had not expected such attention when I arrived and since it was not indeed forthcoming, I followed the porter along the length of the train, past the great, still-breathing engine, and into the station.

Fritz was standing far across the waiting room at the door of the station-master's office, his trench coat unbuttoned, hanging open. Joanna stood a step away from him: a gesture of almost formal detachment. She was already nearly as tall as he was, wearing a navy pea coat that hit her somewhere above the knees, a pair of dark trousers tucked into what appeared to be short rubber boots. A blue wool watch cap was rolled up above her ears and pushed forward, square across her forehead. Her hands were thrust into her coat pockets, her collar turned up against the rain.

She was watching the arrival gates and, when she saw me, turned and made some brief comment to her father and then walked quickly through the crowd to where I was standing. She stood for a moment without a word. Then, with what seemed some difficulty, she said, "Aunt Beatrice, I have the car right in front for you. Out of the rain." She said no more, but with the uneasiness, the strain in her voice, and the unexpected contradiction of it in her intense blue gaze, her appropriation of the moment was complete. She was no longer the slight, diffident twelve-year-old with long blonde hair I had remembered.

Fritz strode up immediately, with a red-cap at his heels. As he held my coat for me, he went to some length to explain why my train was late, matters then quite irrelevant and, I thought, evasive.

Joanna had moved a few paces ahead, walking with the porter, when he added, "We've had over nine inches of rain since yesterday morning. Worst since 'thirty-eight. You haven't had it so bad up around Duluth."

"Yes, I did rather come into town the hard way. I'm afraid this constant rain left little enough to divert my concerns."

I don't recall having actually spoken to either of them up to that point, gestures tentative and too common to be expressive of anything at all being appropriate to a situation neither Fritz nor his daughter seemed quite ready to acknowledge.

"Well, everything's under control now," Fritz said, and lit a cigar with a gesture of impatience and the distraction of searching for an ashstand. He dropped the spent match on the floor.

"It must have been rather a long wait for you," I remarked.

Joanna turned to face us, walking backwards for a few steps, smiling a little for the first time, her hands still pushed deep into the pockets of her coat. "We just got here," she said. "Father checked out the train with the station-master at Hinkley."

Fritz turned and looked at her for a moment and took the cigar out of his mouth. Holding it between his fingers, he gestured to the porter with importunate instructions about putting my luggage into the car as we stepped outside. Joanna glanced at me and then gave the porter a folded bill she took from her coat pocket. Her expression was composed, contained, and touched with what seemed a highly practiced irony.

The rain was still falling heavily as we drove up Hennepin Avenue from the station. Joanna drove, Fritz sat turned in the front seat, his left elbow resting on the back, his fingers clasped together. We had exchanged a few more oblique remarks when he asked Joanna to stop at the smoke shop in the Nicollet Hotel as he was out of cigars. This seemed to me to be a matter that he could surely have attended to earlier. It had been a long and vexing trip into a situation that was bound to be difficult in the days ahead, and I was anxious to arrive at the house.

Tired and annoyed though I was, I could not help but notice Joanna's casual efficiency as she maneuvered the car through a crush of noisy traffic, confusing lights, and the incessant rain. She pulled the car into the cab stand in front of the hotel and leaving the engine running, jumped out, dodged a cab pulling in, moved with noticeable grace over the water flooding the curb, and went into the glass-fronted tobacco shop. She did all this with an ease and a willingness that belied any possibility that the rain had prevented it being done earlier.

"Fritz, how is Maria?"

"There's nothing more to do now."

"Then why did you bring her home?"

"Because she asked to come home." He was silent for a moment and then he added, "Doctors say a few months more. But you can't tell. Could be a lot longer than that. She'll be more comfortable at home." Except for his allusion that Maria's doctors could be in error, he recited this with little apparent conviction.

The rain drummed relentlessly on the glass roof of the cab stand as I watched Joanna inside the tobacco shop. She took off the watchcap and slapped it against her leg to shake off the rain, and ran her fingers through her short hair. I cannot say that I was surprised at how remarkably handsome she had become; just disturbed, I suppose. Prettiness is more easily dismissed. She was smiling and talking quite cheerfully with the tobacconist. She tucked the box of cigars under her arm and at that point he handed her two packages of cigarettes which she pushed quickly into her coat pocket. Yet, she seemed in no great hurry to return to the car.

"I would scarcely have known Joanna. She's changed rather a lot in three years, Fritz."

"Joanna is solid. She's just growing up, that's all."

To me, there seemed a great deal more to it, even on that brief re-acquaintance. "How do you think she's handling this?"

"She's solid, Bea. Joanna's learned to face things." He leaned back against the door of the car. "She knows how things have been."

"Has she told you that?"

He unbuttoned the top button of his coat, but he did not reply. Of course, it sometimes happens that fifteen-year-old girls must face a mother's death. That Joanna had, I assumed, faced it alone for the past year and was doing so hourly now, was a condition he seemed unable to imagine. To assess her as solid may well have solaced him, but it was also a failure of perception I had at least half-expected.

Fritz said nothing more until Joanna left the shop, turning her collar up again against the rain. She was no longer smiling. She handed the box of cigars to her father and drove quickly out onto the avenue. Changing over to the parkway along the river, we drove for the most part in silence relieved only by the slap of the windshield wipers and Fritz's remark that it was getting colder. The rain had begun to turn to sleet. Once, I was acutely aware that Joanna was watching me in the rear view mirror. It occurred to me, with some uneasiness, that had she appeared less cold, less controlled, even less selectively cheerful, I would have been allowed an appropriate sorrow. As it was, her manner clearly challenged such simple convention.

* * * * *

Late that night, finishing the pot of tea I had asked to be sent up to me, I considered, with some bemusement, the lack of portent in the leaves gathered at the bottom of my cup. Portent lay, rather, in Fritz's inconsequent remarks, the diverting errand for cigars invented, I supposed, to waylay any comment from Joanna. But she was commenting. With every gesture, with her strained and mocking silences; a soundless aggression that was both challenge and ironic dismissal of her father.

Strong tea is now my own particular madeleine. It still recalls the revealing weeks of Maria's final illness. She died of acute alcoholism in an obliterating haze of opiates, just before Christmas of that year, giving up with little apparent regret a short, shallow, outwardly amiable life that asked little of her and allowed less. Comfort, as Fritz had so belatedly thought to introduce; comfort, in the sense of one's being at ease about one's self, of fitting well into one's world, is something I doubt Maria Becker had had a great deal of in all her married life.

She was, rather, a spectator of his life, of Joanna's as he shaped it, and of her own only when she was infrequently acknowledged to have one distinct from theirs. Yet, upon her own, she had obviously not been fond of gazing. That she appeared to have accepted all this, dwelling with an indifferent lassitude in the escape so agreeably available to her, was a convenience to Fritz's conscience to the extent that he had one, a justification for awarding all responsibility for such a choice to her, and a corruption they both shared. Unresistant, self-effacing, and denying even an attractive prettiness that could have been enhanced had she had that sense to make the most of natural advantage, Maria simply allowed her life to happen. Except for one brief interlude which I had imagined to be uncharacteristic of her.

A year or so before her marriage to Fritz Becker, she had spent some time in Europe traveling with her parents. She had, ultimately, quarreled with them, and remained in Paris living in a situation which generated alarm and anger in them, but their shock and disapproval was not a factor in altering it. Time, rather, and the unfortunate fitfulness of Maria's brief independence, was.

To suggest that Maria had lacked reasonable purpose in her life is to acknowledge her ultimate denial of any need for one of her own choosing. Now, calmly resigned, and seemingly possessed of no sense of being an impending loss to anyone, she left me with a depressing awareness of her failure. I wanted to hold to some sense of loss; of the destruction, the frustration of potential. But I was left with only concurrence.

Fritz was as I had always known him to be. A reserved, not unpleasant, but sometimes moody man, very involved with the business he had inherited and developed with conspicuous success. This company produced industrial optics during the Great War at the time his grandfather ran the business, and later gunsights of all kinds, naval periscopes and bombsights. Toward the end of the Second War, this enterprise required less personal attention from Fritz, and he began to pursue again those things that obviously interested him.

He was tall, muscular, rather ruddy and even-featured with that frequent blankness of expression presumed to mask depth of mind. A devoted outdoorsman, skilled at riding, shooting and hunting, he spent a great deal of time and money on these things, for himself and for his family. On their home, their cars, and several horses which were boarded at stables a few miles up the river, and on anything else any of them felt they needed.

All this served an image of financial success and a responsible fidelity to the demands of class and position while at the same time separating him from his wife with the usual social impunity. Maria's care for the past year had been progressively taken over by doctors and finally, at this extreme point, by her nurse. And Fritz was free to return to his most absorbing interest, Joanna.

Their only child, she had really been his greatest concern. With her, he was lavish, discriminating, and demanding. From the time she was five or six, he had taken charge of her. With an ostensible devotion to Joanna's care, the control he had assumed over Maria at the outset of their marriage was transferred to his daughter. He designed his own interests to be Joanna's as well, and she ceased to be her mother's daughter.

He taught her to swim, to ride, and to drive a car; to handle guns and boats and to love the outdoors. Not that she didn't seem to enjoy it all quite openly. But I could not set aside my concern for all those choices of the intellect that seemed excluded. All this attention had a certain oddness about it as well; an insensitivity about encouraging the kind of self-assurance, the self-pride that is considered unattractive in a girl. He seemed unaware of how she would use this, or how she might be obliged to transform it into something else once she was brought face to face with its inadmissability. Or just how that would affect her choice.

He and Joanna would often get into long conversations at the dinner table on the fine points of some duck or pheasant hunt. They would review the conditions of the day, the nature of the game, carefully analyzing their own performances to determine how best to achieve perfection the next time they went out. It was an exchange of respect, acknowledgment and belonging.

Until he would equate her with himself. When that happened, she would suddenly, without word or sound, seem to shift the object of her gaze and be looking into a kind of untemporal distance, a private terrain to which only she had access, a preserve where she was sequestering a particular vision of herself and from which he was totally excluded.

Joanna's reserve was both a calculated, mocking barrier of mirrors turned out to reflect the impotence of whoever thought to breach it, and a door to be recklessly opened when she chose. Our conversations during all those long weeks were guided by her into generalities; noncommittal and evasive. Watchful, wary, often with a surprising, ironic humor, she kept them deliberately exclusionary. Except one, the day her mother died.

* * * * *

On that first night two years ago, much of this I was yet to discover. Finishing my tea, aware of the silence in the house, I was aware, too, of the ambiguities in the entire situation, a very real sense of disturbance between Fritz and his daughter. Joanna did not impress me as growing up particularly solid at all. My mind was so clear on this point, that I was unaware for some moments that her imagined voice, repeating her few brief remarks made earlier in the evening, had become quite actual, accusative and unmistakably angry as she argued with Maria's nurse at the head of the stairway.

I placed my cup quietly in its saucer and went to my open door. Joanna was walking directly toward her mother's room. The nurse, carrying a small tray covered with a white napkin, was moving quickly, but without success, to stay ahead of her and reach the door first. With her hand on the knob, Joanna turned. She was still wearing the same dark trousers rolled up at the cuffs, and a heavy white sweater. She was in her stocking feet. In the deeply shadowed light from the stairway, she appeared, for the first time, pale, disturbed, and abruptly older than she was.

"What difference does it make if I see her. If I talk to her. What difference does it make now," she said.

"Your father has forbidden it."

"That doesn't make any difference either." And she went into her mother's room, closing the door quietly behind her. I did not hear her return to her own rooms that night.

* * * * *

By morning, a first light snow had fallen, dusted the bluffs and the hills across the river and moved on. The sky had cleared to a still, cold blue, and I stood for a few moments with my robe gathered around me watching the river flow in dark indifference under the sheen of a pale lemon sun. At eight o'clock, since no other hour had been suggested, I went downstairs for breakfast. Fritz's suitcase, his coat and hat and briefcase were stacked at the foot of the stairway across from the study door. He and Joanna were already at the table in the breakfast room, and he folded his paper and set it aside as I came in.

"Morning, Bea. Sit over here, the view is better." And he reached out to move a place setting across the table. Thus, I sat looking out over a small dormant apple orchard, the sunlight fusing it into a haze of bare branches as it descended the slope at the side of the house. Joanna had left her chair and gone to the sideboard where she poured me a cup of coffee and refilled her own. She paused with a cup in either hand, asked with marked politeness whether I used cream and sugar, and when I declined both, she smiled, apparently to herself, placed my cup at my right hand, took a swallow from her own again, and with the same deliberate courtesy asked if I wanted eggs and how would I like them prepared.

She went to the serving pantry door, leaning in for a moment arranging for my breakfast. Standing with her back to me, still holding her coffee cup in one hand, she shifted her weight with what seemed a conscious awareness of her own easy grace, and crossed one ankle over the other. I hadn't noticed before that she was wearing a pair of twill riding pants, a shirt, and flat-heeled boots.

"Aunt Beatrice," she remarked, turning back to the table, "I didn't ask if you liked them scrambled with cream and Romano." She said this without any marked concern about it and added, "They're one of Father's culinary innovations he brought back from Chicago." She returned to her breakfast without looking at me again, but at her last remark, which had come on a dry shift of tone in her voice, Fritz glanced at her and paused for a moment before he resumed spreading butter on his piece of toast.

I said, "You're leaving town, Fritz."

"Just checking out some re-tooling in the Chicago plant, Bea."

"I should think you'd be sending someone else at this time."

He looked at me with the piece of toast halfway to his mouth, and shook his head.

"No. I need everybody else at this end."

"It's unfortunate there's no one else you can rely on now."

"Right now, I need to be in Chicago."

"Yes, with the war over I suppose new priorities are difficult for you to set."

He finished the last of his toast and sat forward suddenly in his chair, pulling the napkin from his lap. He glanced at the newspaper and folded it and held it in his hand.

"Priorities aren't the problem," he said.

"Perhaps it only seemed so to me, Fritz. I am thinking of Maria."

He looked at me with an expression of rather blank annoyance at having something recalled to him at an inappropriate time. "Bea, I've talked to Lindqvist, and I can be reached if it's necessary." It was the first time he had mentioned Maria's doctor by name, and I felt his use of it as less a reassurance to me than justification for himself.

Joanna had finished her breakfast and was playing with a butter knife, making cross-hatchings on her folded napkin, seemingly absorbed in the pattern being created. Without looking up, she said, "I've been assigned to be your tour guide, Aunt Beatrice. A few things have changed at least. Two new horses at the stable, and the boat house is finished now. And I can drive you into town whenever you like."

Fritz pushed his chair back from the table, then looked at Joanna for a moment waiting to get her attention. "Your real job is to check out that new duck boat before I get back." She nodded, but made no other reply. "We'd better get moving, or I'll miss my train." And he left the table and went quickly into the study.

Joanna refolded her napkin and set the knife carefully beside it. "I have to take Father to the station, but I should be back in an hour. Then we'll do whatever you like." She looked at me for a moment, probably anticipating what had crossed my mind, and said, "I don't have to get back to school until next week for finals."

"I want to go up and talk with your mother this morning, Joanna."

"Yes," she said. "I want her to know you're here now." She stood up, then ran a hand through her hair. "I want her to know," she said again, and went upstairs.

There are, I have found, few reliable guided tours to the internal changes any of us experience. The chips and scars we carry simply record their passage. What further Joanna intended that her mother should know must still have lain quite carefully hidden from both of them. It was not the first time she would raise such allusions, safe in the knowledge that circumstances of the moment would prevent any further exposure.

Winter's first warning passed. Indian Summer polished the clear blue mornings and shortened the afternoons in a golden haze of remembrance and burning leaves. With Fritz away, Joanna wore her mantle of reserve less tightly held. Although she often took the car and drove off in the mornings, or disappeared on afternoons into the quiet of the upstairs, our dinners together and coffee afterward in front of the fire gradually became open, and at times easy, explorations for her. Her moods, her careful manipulation of our conversations, her quick thrusts into my thoughts and parryings to guard her own, were both cautionary signal and invitation.

One morning before breakfast, I went out for a solitary walk along the narrow blacktop road that led away from the house. Years before the first World War, Fritz's grandfather had cleared a point high on the bluff and built the great brick English house with its back to the river. Now, the acres surrounding it were thick with spruce and sugar maple and tall, thin poplar trees had forced their way up through a tangle of hawthorne, wild roses and shadbush.

As I left the road to follow a narrow bridle path, the morning sun silently cleared the river bluff, dappled light casting into relief the pattern of a single horse's tracks going toward the house. Intent on them, knowing that only Joanna could have come that way as silent and self-possessed as the sun itself, I quickened my pace, startling a partridge out of a patch of prickly gorse directly in front of me. The bird rose straight up, then wheeled, flashing low and unerringly through the tangle of brush, the trace of sudden flight lost in a moment as the leaves settled into silence again. Near the edge of the apple orchard, the path ended. At some earlier time, she must have ridden on to the house, but the tracks I was following stopped and then folded back upon themselves.

Divided by a cedar block walk, the back lawn, dry and uneven, bordered by beds of stiff, shaggy purple asters and a few marigolds, was sequestered by the two wings of the house stretching out to the river. On one side was the upstairs suite where I had finished my pot of tea the night I arrived; across it, Joanna's wing, her sitting room overlooking the river. The walk led to a flight of wooden steps descending to the dock below.

Going down through the deep red sumac covering the bluff down to the river's edge, I saw the boathouse built out over the water. On the narrow white canvas covered dock, a freshly painted green canoe, two polished paddles beside it, lay inverted to the sun. Inside the boathouse, a small motorboat tethered on a knotted rope swung with the current, its hull scarred along the bow. A flat duckboat, wrapped in a tight tarpaulin, hung in shadow overhead.

I gazed at it for a moment while the river flowed and broke in a quiet eddy under the dock and the boat pulled out on its rope and swung back again. Quickly, I stepped back out into the sunshine and saw Joanna standing at the top of the steps.

"You're up early," she called and half ran down the steps.

"It's too lovely a morning to be sleeping."

"I can't either. Sleep late, I mean."

Her khaki pants were cut off at the knees, but she rolled them up a couple of times and kicked off her sandals. She gathered up the canoe paddles and, stepping off the dock into the water, stowed them along a rack half way up the wall inside the boathouse. With one quick grasp, she righted the canoe and lowered it into the water. Floating it inside, she lifted it onto a lower padded rack, and washed her hands in the water.

"It's not as heavy as it looks," she said through a quick, almost apologetic smile.

"Should the other boat be left in the water?"

"It's Father's. He'll do what he likes with it." She stepped up on the dock, picked up her sandals, and with her wet footprints running after her on the white canvas, stopped at the bottom of the steps.

"Breakfast should be ready, Aunt Beatrice. I thought maybe you would like to drive up to the stables afterward. And see the new horses."

The barn was warm with the sweet fragrance of hay and grain, a musk of oats and barley and clean horses, leather deep with saddle soap, and the sharp, astringent smell of liniment. The cedar block floor laid down between the stalls on either side had been freshly hosed down and the late morning sun slanting through the wide open doors glinted off the runnels of water still standing between the blocks. At the far end, the trap to the loft was open over a wooden ladder nailed to the wall, and someone was pitching hay above. At the edge, a yellow cat sat looking down at us and then quietly walked away through the sunlit motes of dust drifting to the floor below.

I stopped by the tack room door and watched Joanna as she walked down the stalls pausing to share a whinnied greeting, to stroke a horse along the neck, ending her touch with a gentle slap, offering a lump of sugar flat in her hand, and then moving on as the horses turned in their boxes, rustling the fresh straw underfoot, hanging their heads over the gates, quietly watching her pass.

As she came back along the opposite stalls, I realized, unmistakably then, how aware she was of her own untutored grace, how much she enjoyed it. She was totally at ease with her body — with its unconscious expression of harmony with the state of her mind, with an untroubled assessment of herself formed in the emotional sanctuary she had of necessity made. For that moment, she seemed to exist only for herself. And yet I felt she knew, with a tangible, physical certainty, what she was creating. For that moment, she had invaded me completely, just as I know now she had intended to do.

She smiled and came up quickly, stopping to slap the rump of a fine-boned chestnut mare standing with alert patience outside the stalls, its head held high and pulling taut the light chains attached to the halter and stretched to either side across the corridor.

"Her name is Flying Dutchess. She's my best girl," Joanna said. "Aren't you?" she added, and went into the tack room.

The mare rolled an eyeball back, watching Joanna as she came back with the saddle on her arm, the bridle slung over her shoulder. She stroked the horse again and pulled the saddle cloth up toward her withers and put the saddle on her back, the girth hanging loose, the stirrup irons still drawn up. While she unsnapped the two chains, Joanna and her mare were engaged in a small conversation, and after a moment she removed the halter and slipped the bit into the horse's mouth and pulled the bridle on. She smiled as she pulled the mare's ears and set the band over her forelock, and then tossed the reins over her neck. Only then did she fasten the cinch, slip the stirrups down, then draw the cinch tight once again.

Joanna rode on ahead, trotting the mare along a dirt path that led to a long oval course beyond the stables. I crossed a small field of cropped grass and clover where the track of the mower wound past clumps of blue cornflowers and long grass gone to tassle. The course, laid out for competition with rail and brush jumps, walls and gates and triple bars, was shaded by a long row of poplar trees. The small grandstand where Joanna had suggested I sit was built just in front of the trees. A slim, tow-headed youngster with a deep red tan and wearing a cowboy hat, was sitting on the bottom steps. He stood up as I approached, touched the brim of his hat to me, and walked over to talk to Joanna who was pointing to first one and then another of the jumps. He stepped through the white rail fence around the course and busied himself moving rails and kicking at brush on the jumps she had indicated, while she walked her horse along the fence and turned in at the start of the course.

Impatient, the mare turned her ears forward, threw her head up and pivoted suddenly, raising a small cloud of dust. Joanna leaned forward and touched her neck, wheeled her slowly around to steady her. They took the first brush and double rails with no more than a necessary, confident room to spare. Rounded the curve leaving another rail wobbling but settling back above the first low wall jump, and went on to complete the figure eight through a cluster of green and white checker-patterned bars and small pointed flags fluttering on the posts. Finishing the eight, they bore back to the outside of the track. Only once again did they nick a rail, and then cleared the water jump with nothing at all to spare while the boy in the cowboy hat, leaning against the fence on the other side of the course, watched critically.

The mare refused at the final double jump and gate. She turned against the bars, down on her haunches, but Joanna kept her seat, reined her in, steadied her, and took her back to try again. They cleared it then, came around the curve and into the last diagonal with an impatience they both seemed to share, and returned to the start in a slow,

measured trot. On the second try, Joanna took her
mare through the course without a flaw. Then she
trotted Flying Dutchess out along the fence and
stopped in front of me.

"That was just to prove we could do it. Wasn't it,
girl?" And Joanna stroked the mare's neck with
affection, kicked her right foot out of the stirrup,
and crossed her leg over the pommel of the saddle.

"I didn't really doubt it. How long have you been
doing this?"

Joanna looked at me carefully for a moment, and
then she smiled. "Jumping, Aunt Beatrice? Or
proving it?"

"Both, I expect."

"I've been at it for almost three years now. But
Dutchess has only just begun. At least with me."

"That's proved it as far as your father is
concerned, I trust."

"No, I'm sure it hasn't. He didn't want me to buy
her. Said she wasn't sound." Joanna slipped her
other foot out of the stirrup and jumped down in
what I felt sure she had been told was a quite
unacceptable way to dismount. "Dutchess comes from
a good breed line. We get along just fine." And she
slipped the stirrup irons up and held the reins in
one hand.

We walked together then, back along the path to
the stables, Dutchess content to walk a step or two
off Joanna's left side. Occasionally she would shake
her head, her light bridle rattling, and nuzzle
Joanna's shoulder. With the sun low behind us, our
long shadows moved ahead on the path. Beyond the
stables, the Indian Summer haze lay over a field of
stubble and shocked corn, and the broken trails of

dried and withered pumpkin vine. The air had cooled
and grown still. I folded my arms against my body
and held them there, watching the sand of the path
drift across my shoes. And I realized how difficult it
had been for me to admire with more than
perfunctory remarks the new horses Joanna had
shown me earlier in the stable.

I don't ride, but I do find good horses beautiful. I
enjoy watching them, and I admire those who handle
them well. Joanna had surprised me. Like her
remarks, unguarded and bluntly honest, and then
carefully innocuous, so skilled a show seemed a
deliberate effort to both mask and to reveal more
than I had thought she wanted me to see. Yet it
seemed to me, too, an incongruous and even
arrogant display of special virtues learned from an
indulgent father. That I knew I was judging Joanna
quite unfairly, as beyond her years, both annoyed me
and hardened my opinion of Fritz.

"It's less than generous of your father to question
your judgment about the horse. Or should I say
unfair, Joanna?"

She looked at me, surprised as much, I suppose,
because I had broken the long silence, as at my
question. But she said nothing and gathered the
reins up in her hand to hold Dutchess close under
the bridle.

"Particularly because you handle her so well," I
added.

"Aunt Beatrice, I like doing things well. It's
important to me. And Father has taught me to do a
lot of things well."

Joanna handed the mare over to the stable boy
in the cowboy hat, told him to rub her down

carefully and put a blanket on her. We walked to the car. She glanced at me, my arms still folded. "I've an extra jacket in the car," she said, and smiled in a speculative, rather rueful sort of way as she helped me slip into it.

Driving back along the river, we passed through still-brilliant yellow poplar growing thick to the edge of the blacktop road, standing so close together it seemed impossible that one could penetrate their ranks. The shifting pattern of their leaves was spattered red by the sumac covering the bluff beyond. Neither of us spoke for several minutes. Joanna drove slowly, her hands resting on the top of the wheel, her two thumbs just touching at the tips of the nails. Occasionally she took her eyes off the road and pushed her thumb tips firmly together as though she were mentally drawing a baseline on the little triangle that resulted, the necessary completion of the pattern.

It was impossible to believe that she was unaware of my scrutiny, her pose of indifference not so formidable to challenge it as was simply too evanescent to assault. Once again, she seemed perfectly protected by some unique coloration of her own.

"I'd better start checking out the duck boat before dinner," she said suddenly.

"Yes, I expect so. Your father will be home tomorrow night and he did seem rather insistent about that."

"He usually is about things like that."

Other quite different things, like his stricture against disturbing Maria, were apparently distinct in

Joanna's mind from concerns upon which she and her father agreed.

I said, "I'm afraid I've always thought duck boats to be less than safe."

Joanna bit her lower lip and then turned and smiled at me with a small mixture of agreement and indulgence. "However you want to look at it. But it does help to make sure it folds for hauling, unfolds without ripping the skin, and that all the gear is in place. And," she said, taking a deep breath, "that it's been water-tested in the river, and that it's repacked and ready to go when he gets back." She recited this in the resigned voice of a camp counsellor, yet unable to disguise a small note of pride.

Ready to go when? To ask that question was to exercise one of those pointed little deceits in conversation, those ornamental evasions we so confidently expect will invite commitment.

"You know already, don't you, Aunt Beatrice. Duck season opens the end of next week and Father and I will be going up to Deerwood for ten days."

"I'm not surprised that your father finds it appropriate to go now, no."

She was gripping the top of the steering wheel with both hands, and without looking at me, she leaned back relaxing her grip, and with a free hand reached into her jacket pocket for a cigarette, lighting it from the lighter on the dash. Because I said nothing more, or perhaps to intercept it, she pushed the lighter back into place and said, "We've been going to Deerwood every opening day since I was nine. Father gave me a four-ten for my birthday then. Last year was the first time he let me handle a twelve-gauge. I learned a lot of things on that trip."

"You're very fortunate," I said. "In that respect."

"In what respect?"

"That your father includes you with his friends. That he's devoted himself to that, of course."

"He's taught me what he likes, if that's what you mean."

Joanna smoked her cigarette in silence without apparently intending any further elaboration. She may have wondered why I made no comment on her smoking without her father's knowledge, but little at that point suggested that either my disapproval or concern weighed heavily with her.

She put out the cigarette with particular care, and there was a marked change in her voice. "Aunt Beatrice, once when I was little, I asked my mother what the stars were made of, and I remember that she laughed and held me at a distance and said it didn't matter because no one would ever get there."

"That was hardly a satisfactory answer."

"No, it wasn't. Though I understand it better now."

"Yes, I expect you do."

"It satisfied her."

I wondered at the dismissive edge in her remark, yet nothing marred her cool, controlled look, as though she allowed nothing to betray pure patrician features that bore no trace of her father's coarseness, nor Maria's dark ruin. We had reached the short, winding drive up to the house, and I realized as Joanna shifted gears that once again she had measured her remarks with consummate skill against time and circumstance. It became my choice to extend time; to at least shift circumstance.

"You're with your mother often at night."

"My mother didn't tell you that."

"No, Joanna. You did, the night you argued with her nurse outside my door."

She pulled the car up to the side entrance. The engine died into silence and her small sigh hung for a moment on the air. She made no move to leave the car.

"I don't know what the woman was doing out there that late," she said. "But you heard the whole thing anyway."

"Not entirely, no."

"Aunt Beatrice, Father asked you to come here because of Mother. He wanted it that way. He needed it, I guess." She sat up suddenly and pulled the key from the ignition. "I accepted that," she said, and pulled sharply at the handle of the door beside her. "That's enough, isn't it?"

As the latch sprung loose, she paused and let the door fall gently to again. "I went in to read to her. We've been doing that for a long time now. Late at night. Sometimes she's asleep, but I read to her anyway. Or to myself."

"Your father doesn't know about this, does he?"

"I don't think it matters to him."

"What matters to him is hardly my concern."

"Which means all this has a whole lot to do with me, doesn't it?"

"Yes, and with Maria's concern for you. That is what she talks to me about."

"It's not my mother who should worry about that. Or about me."

"I don't accept that."

"Accept what, Aunt Beatrice?" She looked at me
for a moment and shook the car keys in her hand.
"Why not? You asked me a minute ago if Father
knows I spend so much time with my mother. No,
he doesn't know about it. He doesn't know anything
about her, and there's a lot more he doesn't know
about me. I'm not sure anyone needs to."

Fritz's return at the end of that week was oddly
celebrational. The weather had turned crisp and
invigorating, and his usual good spirits, apparently
heightened by the prospect of the duck season,
brought a not totally inappropriate glow to the
house. It would have taken a far firmer resolve than
my own not to have welcomed some relief from the
concern, the sorrow that I, at least, felt should then
be the main burden of their lives. As for Joanna,
her reaction seemed one of relief that he had at last
returned, and that action would again move the
days.

Fritz had evidently suggested that changes be
made in the way the house was being run, that
some notably absent amenities be restored. That
evening, the fireplace in the living room was bright
with a big log fire, the lamps were lit, and the doors
to the den opened wide to the fire glowing on that
hearth as well. Across the entryway, the dining room
table was set for the three of us, the crystal warmed
by the firelight and a dusky glow from the linen.
The candles were ready to be lit.

Fritz was mixing drinks at a small mahogany

liquor cabinet, and he and Joanna were apparently discussing this as I came in.

"Well, I'm pretty sure your Aunt Beatrice will agree with me," he said, and turned to me. "She's going to be sixteen in a few weeks, and I say that's old enough to start celebrating with a small drink."

I conceded, "A small one, I suppose."

"Bea, you're up to a martini, aren't you?"

Joanna was looking at me with an understandable confusion of surprise and doubt. While I found myself concerned that she would decide to add the clandestine cigarettes to her father's version of adulthood, I believe I was challenged far more by the fact that she had changed for dinner.

Her easy, careless lapse from that stricture while Fritz was away had been constrained by a slim, belted skirt, the required heels and a short, perfunctory strand of matched pearls. But her silk shirt was open low at the neck with a show of arrogance that I couldn't help feeling was an appeal not to her father, but to me; as though she were testing some new awareness of herself and to a purpose not without its ambiguity. Fritz seemed not to notice. He handed her the drink he had mixed in a tall, frosted glass, gave me my martini and then raised his own glass.

"To growing up," he said, smiling at Joanna. She looked at him, and in the firelight the clear lines of her face took on more gravity, a slight movement raised her chin, and she seemed to see not him, but beyond. In an instant, she came back.

"Yes, to growing up," she answered, and she smiled broadly and added, "Maybe I'll try that."

The comfort in the room, the fire, the drinks, and

Fritz's conversation about Chicago and the results of
his trip kept some thirty minutes or so at an
amiable level. At one point, he dismissed with
conventional asperity "this fellow Truman — he'll
finish up the term and that's all," adding with
assurance that the previous administrations might
claim to have won the war, but American business
would build the future. It was difficult not to hear
the *Chicago Journal of Commerce* in all this with its
marked avoidance of Roosevelt's name. His
unbreathed sigh at the narrow escape from Mr.
Wallace's ascendancy seemed better left without
comment.

If his reference to the coming duck season was
intended to elicit some favorable sign from Joanna, it
was unavailing. She had moved to a wing chair by
the fire, her long legs straight out, ankles crossed,
one elbow on the arm of the chair, holding her glass
carefully in one hand. She sipped occasionally from
it, watching her father most of the time, maintaining
without comment a rather studied attention to his
remarks. And he watched her while he talked. But
with an uneasy air of puzzlement, a certain lack of
the certitude he had always shown. It was at such a
moment that dinner was announced, and he slapped
his knee as though to break the mood. "Good," he
said, as he stood up. "After dinner I have something
special for you." And he turned and held his hand
out to Joanna. She rose without taking it.

Dinner that evening was a meal warm at first,
with moderated good feeling and a comfortable
extension of the conversation to include the city of
Duluth and the changes I had seen since the war's
end. Then, with an air of appropriation he did not

expect to be challenged, Fritz turned the conversation to duck hunting. His and Joanna's concerns with it, and an examination of her skills, probing and critical.

Both praised and damned, she was being exposed in a situation that I expect was no more trying than many others that had been their private and mutual concern in the past. Nevertheless, she bore it well, I thought. Despite her small drink and the almost empty wine glass, she reacted with grace, self assurance, and a kind of cold, disquieting calm. And, with a thin, challenging edge in her voice, often touched with an amusement I sensed to be something untried before.

Fritz had been expounding on the general conditions of duck hunting in a manner suggesting his satisfaction in his own fund of knowledge rather than whatever importance there was in it to convey to Joanna. "Every bird that migrates through here funnels down into the Mississippi Flyway, and most of them winter in Arkansas' Grand Prairie. You know as well as I do when that begins."

"When the first mare's-tails change the sky, the ducks come. Always."

"October," he said. Joanna shrugged a little, and a smile touched the corners of her mouth. Fritz went on. "Over half the wildfowl coming across this country use our flyway. Mallards, greenwings, canvasbacks, we get them all. Wooducks, pintails, everything from the Western Arctic. Or, as you would say, from the North Hole."

"Maybe the Indians were right; their home is on the other side of the sky." Joanna gathered some wild rice on her fork and paused before putting it in her mouth. "Sometimes, Father, I guess I do like to just watch them."

"That can be pretty dangerous. A duck blind is no place to be dreaming."

"No. It's a place for reading every signal the birds give me." She paused, her fork in her hand, and then she continued, her voice flat, even, and careful. "For knowing that only canvasbacks have short tails and their feet are held flat out behind them when they fly. That greenwings are small and fast and long-winged. That all ducks circle into the wind, into the decoys, and when they drop their tails they are ready to pitch in. That blackjacks and teal come in like gangbusters, and that pintails and mallards, especially mallards, are slow and cautious and circle more."

Joanna put her free right hand flat on the tablecloth, spreading her fingers slowly, and looked up at her father. "Have you ever noticed how fastidious mallards are when they land? How they let the air slip through their flight feathers to set their descent. Hold their wings back so they won't get wet, and then fold them so deliberately as they settle in." And she slowly closed her fingers against the white tablecloth.

"You've learned all that to make you a better shot. To get the limit you're entitled to. That's what you're out there for, as I have to keep reminding you." Fritz carved himself some breast meat from a third duck still on the platter in front of him.

"I know. Crosswind shots are my best shots. Find the target, cluster them if I can. Lead my birds, but not too far. Point my gun, don't aim. Swing with it, squeeze the triggers and follow through. Isn't that right?" Joanna placed her fork carefully on the edge of her plate and leaned back in her chair. "And if she suddenly gets suspicious, if she gets frightened and turns off?"

"Follow her head. Wherever she turns it, that is where she is going to go."

"Yes, I know where she is going to go."

"And that's your lead. That's your shot. You haven't any excuse if you lose her."

"No. No, I don't."

Throughout all this, Fritz sat, of course, at the head of the table, his back to the service pantry door, Joanna at his right. My place was at the foot, in what had always been Maria's chair. She had sat in that chair every evening for the past nine years, watching her hold on her own life dissolve through a deliberate, corrosive pattern of denial of her right to it. In conversations like that one in which, like her, I took no part. Conversations that transported father and daughter into some exclusionary world where theirs were the worthwhile values. Sharing Maria's exclusion that evening, without the pain of her loss, made it no easier for me to overlook, or justify, her own failure, even if I could then account for it. And for the helplessness she had to have felt when confronted with Fritz's hold on Joanna.

Like my own wine glass during that meal, Maria's had always been refilled, her after-dinner coffees accompanied and followed by enough alcohol to reduce her mind and erase the loss of her marriage, her daughter, and herself. She must have hated him.

Fritz's contempt for his wife had been translated into a neat, socially overlooked contrivance, arrogant

and savage — now complete. It was, as Joanna's
withdrawal, her selective innocence implied, too late
to remedy. Yet, despite Joanna's age, her complicity
was distressingly real. The more so as the reality of
it must have begun to appear to her as unavoidable,
ugly fact. The sense of her own culpability, the
shock of the unimaginable truth of her own loss, was
creating a change in her that Fritz characterized as
growing up. Which indeed it was. But a change not
without a troubling disturbance.

While coffee and dessert were being served,
Joanna moved the conversation to a less adversarial
plane. "These tasted awfully good. I hope what we
get this season will be."

Fritz twisted the stem of his glass in his fingers,
looking at the small disc of wine at the base of the
bowl. He set it down. "They will be. You know the
best eating birds always come from the best feeding
grounds. Why else would we have been replanting
all around Deerwood?"

"Oh," I said. "I've always believed that you
pursued game to its own chosen habitat." Fritz
hesitated for a moment, quite unused, I expect, to
comment from that quarter of the table.

"I think Aunt Beatrice is afraid we're not being
quite sporting," Joanna said.

"Not at all," Fritz was quick to reply. "The more
we preserve and expand feeding grounds all along
the flyway, the more ducks there are. We've always
got to factor in our own efforts." He had finished his
dessert and was turning his coffee cup slowly in the
saucer as he talked. "This time there will be enough
so you don't have to go after the first ones in," he

said to Joanna. "This is the year I'm going to break you of that habit," he added.

"I want to have some coming on behind when I miss," Joanna said, smiling again at what even I knew to be the sort of remark a neophyte would make.

"You're talking like a wade hunter," Fritz said, and the sarcasm in his voice, the implication of hapless foundering in the marsh, defined the term well enough. "They're not going to wait for you, you know. You've got to get out there and line up your ducks. Literally." And he laughed at his own remark.

"Yes, for sure." Joanna turned her dessert spoon in her fingers and set it upside down on the table.

"I'll grant you, you don't miss often." Fritz smiled at her for the first time. "You're just inconsistent. Like you were last year. Your limit on six doubles in one morning. All the rest of the time you were scatter shooting into the wind."

"Maybe I'm just not really that good a shot yet."

"Only when you're daydreaming. You are when you want to be."

Walking beside me back to the living room, Fritz continued with his concentration on what he took to be Joanna's problem. "You should have seen it, Bea. It was pretty hard to believe after a performance like that. The next day when the third flight came in, one drake just hung over the water for a full minute and with that lead, she missed him. And the two hens that followed, one right on the wing of the other. She missed them both."

At this, he laughed. Not, it seemed, in any markedly unkind way. But whatever measure of indulgence was in his laughter was clearly lost to Joanna. She had walked to the fireplace and was standing with her hands on the edge of the mantle, looking down into the coals of the fire. As Fritz poured out three brandies, he continued with what had become a rather disembodied monologue.

"It's hard to figure. She's beautifully coordinated. All her action is firm, natural and decisive like a man's should be."

Joanna turned to look at him, the fire burning up suddenly behind her. "It has to do with how I think about it. About shooting them, I mean. Shooting anything, Father."

I certainly was not prepared to hear her make utterly clear what she had given him every chance to infer in her remarks at the dinner table. The tone in her voice, the same cold calm she had maintained then seemed to startle Fritz. But only for a moment.

His small frown changed quickly to a confident, dismissive smile. "I've got just what it will take to change your mind about that." And he stepped quickly inside the doorway of the den and returned with a long-barreled, thin black shotgun which he placed with an expression of absolute triumph in Joanna's hands.

For the barest moment, she seemed transfixed, hypnotized by the charmer, possessed by his gift; by the gun, alive and poised in serpentine intent in her hands. With a quick, defensive descent into consuming pleasure, she breathed one word in Italian, "Bernardelli," smiling with a kind of relieved joy. And in a gesture of effortless certitude, she balanced the slim gun like a ballerina in her hands as she broke it open, sighted through the long barrels, cleared the chamber, closed the breech and stood turning the gun over and back, holding it easily in one hand, its silver mountings flashing deep with firelight. Her expression changed then; almost, it seemed, with reluctance.

She thanked him, but made no obvious effort to express any further enthusiasm. She was, apparently, quite ready to return to the gravity of manner that this admitted pleasure had invaded. With patience, she let Fritz enjoy the gift he had made. She listened without comment to his redundant recitation of the superiority of the gun, the value of the silverwork, its cost, and the craft that had gone into fitting it to her needs as he had determined them.

Finally, Joanna looked away from him. "Aunt Beatrice, you must think this house is turning into a shooting gallery."

Her statement was not that odd. It would have been amusing had there been amusement in her voice. But with an equal lack of humor, she shifted the gun, holding it straight across her hips. A stance just short of one simple move, one shift of her weight away from bringing it to her shoulder. Fritz had lit a cigar and seemed not to have noticed her abrupt move nor her thin, half-frightened smile. He drew heavily on the cigar and then removed it from his mouth to examine the lighted end of it with practiced care.

"We've a long drive ahead of us tomorrow, young lady. You'd better turn in so we can get out of here by five."

Joanna relaxed her grip on the gun and, holding

it directly vertical, walked with it in one hand into the den where she placed it in the gun rack against the wall.

At the time, I suppose I didn't question whether that thin edge of violence lay in her or in myself. To have disapproved, to have been shocked by it, to have fancied an act of violence from Joanna's insubstantial gesture was an admissable inference. It was quite another thing to finally allow myself the one malignant supposition that exposed the corrosion of their supposedly uncorrupted lives.

Joanna had returned to the fireplace mantle and picked up the small glass of brandy Fritz had poured for her earlier. "I'll be ready and down for some breakfast at four-thirty, if that's all right," she said, glancing at him.

"Okay, lights out."

She stepped off the hearth as though to leave the room, and then she turned and dashed the brandy into the fire. She watched as its peacock flare closed down and then, looking at me, she said, "In a little while. I've some reading yet to do." And she left us.

For the next two days I watched the temperature drop steadily, while gathering winds stripped the leaves from the trees. On the third morning the snow had covered the northern half of the state, moved down the river, and by four o'clock winter had buried the last of fall.

At three the following morning, Maria's nurse woke me to say that her patient had lost consciousness, that the doctor had already been called and was on his way to the house. She also informed me that she did not expect Maria to live beyond that day. Her conclusion proved accurate. Maria died at five-thirty that morning, twenty minutes or so after Doctor Lindqvist's arrival and, I must add, several weeks ahead of her husband's calculations. I called the lodge at Deerwood and asked that Fritz be located.

Fritz called about three o'clock saying that they would leave immediately. Allowing for the heavy snowfall, the drive from Deerwood would take them eight or nine hours. Joanna was fine; she was very strong, he added, though I did not feel it necessary to ask, and did not do so. But I remember experiencing an odd sense of relief, of vindication, after I hung up.

I ate a solitary but not unpleasant dinner in the again dimly lit dining room, Maria's nurse having asked that she be allowed to leave until Mr. Becker returned. Her request seemed an expression of considerable tact which I gratefully took advantage of, although I could, undoubtedly, have learned a great deal from a dinner conversation. Foregoing that, I asked that my coffee be brought to the living room where I poured myself a brandy and sat alone by the fire in the wing chair Joanna had occupied three nights before, so relentlessly suppressing all that she could not yet let loose.

I leaned back into the chair, the black coffee hot in the cup, warming my hand. Save for one lamp I had left lit on the far side, the room was dark, the silence disturbed only by the wavering flare of the fire, the occasional hiss of burning pitch, the sense of wind outside, and the endlessly falling snow.

There is a particular kind of silence that shapes
a house when illness defines it. Attitudes and
necessary functions set capricious but unquestioned
limits, and the silence allows for no further
explanation. It is honored, for transience is its one
promise; interruption its greatest hazard. A death
becomes the voice of silence. And I knew that
Maria's death would speak without sound in
graceless reminders through days of professional
arrangements routinely followed and over which no
approval from her had been sought.

Little that Maria had said to me revealed more
than an unbearable awareness of her own hurt. Each
particular instance of it had become immediate and
shattering, as though she had compressed all the
years of its unrelenting destructiveness into the last
hours of her existence. She knew the source of that
destruction, and she knew its power over her. And
in her final despair, she knew her daughter only as
she knew herself.

Helpless beyond the end, Maria had died with a
tardy sense of concern for her daughter
unaccompanied by any awareness of her strengths.
And uncomprehending of her own great hold on
Joanna — that she was loved by her, unjudged for
the utter bleakness of her failures, raged against in
troubled sorrow. The great knot of emotions would,
as Joanna unravelled it, be her only sanctuary.

Joanna herself was troubling me far more, and
far differently than had the short-spoken, wary girl I
had faced scarcely six weeks before. My uneasiness,
my sense of the peril that lay in the tension

between Joanna and her father was intruding forcibly.

Agony, should there be any, was unquestionably for Fritz to bear. Not for his unacknowledged wrongs against his wife — he would bear none there; but for the painful corruption of his judgment. For the results of it, more correctly. He would lose his daughter. Exposure, undisguised and inescapable for nine more hours would likely affect him little, however much it might finally dispel the last of Joanna's illusions. I felt sure that she had rehearsed this moment of her mother's death often enough, had explored all the possible outcomes of it, and tested all her own reactions. What remained for her was a simple choice and a lifetime of examination of it.

That chance reference to her lifetime made it pointless for me to pretend disinterest beyond the present any longer. To recognize the direction of Joanna's life, the cast of it; to assume justification for control or even influence over it, in short, to challenge Fritz, may have been inadmissible before. It was no longer. That the decision would inevitably reopen a part of my own life seemed, oddly, a minor concern, welcome and perhaps overdue.

With no particular reluctance nor surprise at my lack of it, I found a special pleasure in acknowledging Joanna's gift for economy of both thought and action; her capacity to predetermine the precise degree of reason and efficiency, of grace and gesture required to accomplish what she chose to do. It was an attractive trait. All it wanted was modesty and taste.

The fire had died to bright red coals. One log broke silently, settling into white ash, and the red sparks flew up and disappeared. I glanced at my watch, concerned at the lateness of the hour, and went immediately upstairs.

The draperies in my sitting room were still undrawn, and I walked to the windows without turning on the lights. In the drive below, the wind blew the snow in great curves, drifting it in exaggerations of the porch posts and the open gates farther down the drive. The lamps along the garage doors dimly lit the few bare spots on the dark cedar block paving. Only the clean, unmarked snow covering the lawn and the walk to the service kitchen downstairs relieved the bleakness, while the snow continued to fall.

It seems odd to me now, that scenes of snow are assumed to be silent, a noiseless, unbroken chill. Not the hot, shattering picture that one became the instant the headlights flashed along the bars of the gate and the car stopped.

Fritz was out first, pulling his mittens on as he stepped across the beam of the headlights, the snow scattering like tinsel on his coat. At that moment, Joanna got out of the car and in three steps stood in the center of the snow-covered lawn facing him, the slim black shotgun in her hands. She must have called to him, for he stopped, his hands at his sides, an expression of mild bewilderment on his face that quickly changed to contempt. He spoke to her in words I could only see, and abruptly turned his back and walked to the garage.

It was then that she raised the gun, and on her soundless shout he turned as she threw it, vertical, barrels straight up, leaping like a dying thing across the snow. Instinctively he caught it, and for a moment she stood with her arm still outstretched in a gesture almost of supplication, almost of warding off a blow. Then she picked up the game bag she had dropped at her feet and came into the house through the service kitchen door.

I stood for several minutes looking at echoes of light defining only a pattern of black footprints in the snow. An instant later I heard Joanna running up through the back service stairway. As quickly as I could, I went to the door at the head of the stairwell, and as I reached it, heard her stumble and fall. I opened the door. She was sitting doubled over at the top step, leaning against the wall, her head bent on her arms.

I knelt beside her and put my arm around her shoulder, knowing with a small shock that it was the first time I had touched her. I felt her stiffen, and then she reached up and put her hand over mine.

"Joanna. Will you come in with me for a while?"

Slowly she drew her hand away. She stood up then, a look of inexpressible calm on her face, as though some abstract grief had shaken her but had been spent for now. She was still wearing her hunting coat, and I noticed then that it was stained with blood.

"My ducks," she said, and ran her hand across her coat. "I killed them all."

I turned and walked to my sitting room door and held it open for her.

"May I wash my hands?" And she held them out as though to verify this need, and walked through

my bedroom, carefully shutting the door leading into
the center hall before she went into the bath.

She returned shortly with a towel folded around
her neck, the ends hanging down in front of the red
shirt she wore. She had taken off the coat and was
holding it with some hesitation in one hand, a
gesture of apology, I expect, toward my obvious
distaste. Then she folded it, with the stain covered,
and put it on the chair by the door.

"I had to hurry," she said. "So I carried them in
the bag inside my coat for a while. But I guess you
don't want to hear about it."

"Not about that, no."

She sat down on the foot of the lounge, the towel
still hanging loose around her neck. "I had to
hurry," she repeated. "I didn't want to be left out
there. Father was walking so fast."

"I would think he should have been. The men at
the lodge took the dogs out to find you, didn't they?"

"Yes. We saw the dogs first, and then Olaf Lind
came and told us you'd called. About Mother." She
leaned over and carefully loosened the laces on her
boots before she said anything more. "I didn't know
Father hadn't put our route on the log. He's never
forgotten to do that before. It's like he wanted us
cut off out there. He just picked up the Jeep at the
lodge before dawn and we drove out toward the lake.
Into the marsh as far as he could go. The wind had
let up some, but it was still snowing." She slipped
off the boots, and set them together beside the
lounge. "Enough to cover our tracks," she added.

"They're plain to see now, Joanna."

She glanced at me and then spread her hands

out on her knees, watching them as she carefully flexed her fingers.

"I know you saw us drive in. You saw what happened." She looked at me suddenly. "Aunt Beatrice, I can't listen to him anymore. Telling me what to do, what to think. I just can't do it anymore. What he is thinking —" She reached down to straighten her boots out against the edge of the lounge. "— I just don't know."

"I think you do."

"We walk to the blind and he tells me about the wind. Tells me where the flight will come in. Tells me we'll have cross shots, as if I didn't know all of that. Tells me what to concentrate on."

"On shooting? Is that what you were concentrating on?"

"Aunt Beatrice, that's the last time I will have to shoot them."

"I hope that's the last time you have to shoot anything. I'm talking about your father, Joanna. Is that what you were thinking of doing?"

She sat motionless for a moment, the ends of the towel around her neck held tight in her hands, looking at me with an expression of transparent disbelief.

"God, Aunt Beatrice. No. My God, that's crazy, isn't it?"

"To think it? I'm not so sure of that. In any case, I knew it wouldn't happen."

"You knew."

"You did not?"

Joanna looked at me for a long moment before she answered. "I don't know," she said, and in the silence I could hear her firm, even breathing. "Yes, I did. I knew. It was after I shot my birds. I waited, wondering why he hadn't fired. I reloaded, and it was after that. I saw him push the duck boat out of the other blind up the marsh where he had gone. The boat was weaving a little bit because he doesn't paddle it right. Cutting across to pick up my birds. Like a pattern, like a triangle, until he was right in front of me out on the water. I stood there with my gun. I could have shot him. I don't know why I didn't. I just sat down on the plank bench and took the shells out of my gun."

"The gun he gave you last week."

"Yes. The Bernardelli." She pulled the towel from around her neck and folded it, held between her hands. "He came back finally, carrying the birds. He'd gutted them, and it made me sick. And sorry. It's hard for me to do that. He just threw them over beside my game bag." She took a long, deep breath and said again, "I don't know why I didn't do it. God, I don't know." She looked at me with a small, resigned smile, shook her head, and began the quiet retreat into the shelter of herself I had grown so familiar with. "It wouldn't have been worth it, would it?"

"Joanna, I despise cant. And I especially dislike hearing it from you. It's a very poor deceit that will never disguise what I know you are feeling, what I know you are avoiding."

"My father —" And she stopped.

"Your father will answer for himself when, and if, he becomes my concern."

She doubled the folded towel in her hands and then she set it aside at the end of the lounge. "My father will never answer for himself, Aunt Beatrice." She seemed to be saying this as much to herself as to me, and although she was looking at me directly, she was seeing through and beyond with an air of cautious selectivity. "I've known for a long time what it would be like to feel the way I do now. I'm not sure I can explain it, but it all worked out." She shook her head again, as though she was considering some particularity and had found it better reserved for another time.

"I would expect you to answer only for yourself, Joanna. When you are ready."

"I've been ready for a long time. I just never knew when it would be until this morning. A lot of things suddenly got sorted out."

"That is a natural enough part of growing. All our lives, I'm sure."

She made no immediate reply, seeming again to be examining some brief, private debate in her own mind. "Aunt Beatrice, my mother has been dead for a very long time. I don't know exactly what happened this morning. It doesn't seem to have anything to do with her. It's like she was two people." She ran her hands through her hair and finally held them in her lap, pushing a thumb at the tips of her fingers. "I think I was afraid to love my mother. Somehow, I know, I was told that she was not to be loved. That she didn't love me. I guess I believed that until I began to. To love her. In secret. She was terribly afraid of him. That surprised me until now. She was so sure I didn't understand what was happening. That it would happen to me."

"That, is impossible."

"I wish she could have realized that."

"Do you really understand what was happening?"

Perhaps Joanna's reply was a little quick in coming, but it was accurate.

"Not entirely, no. But enough to know that I'll spend the rest of my life unlearning a lot of things."

She sat for a moment longer, and then she got up and took the towel back to the bathroom. When she returned, she walked to the chair by the door and picked up her hunting coat.

"Maybe it does have something to do with the ducks." She paused and looked at me with a sudden directness as though she half-expected I knew what she was thinking. "I've never really wanted to kill them. That's why I tried so often not to hit them and still make it look good. As long as I could avoid killing them, at least some of the time, Father was safe. If that's not too mixed up. But this morning I knew I had to. I knew exactly what I was going to do. I grouped my ducks and killed all three of them. With two shells. Father never fired a shot. He never said a word to me. We just rode back to the lodge with Olaf and the dogs."

She folded the coat over her arm and opened the door, her hand still on the knob.

"I wish you could have seen how lovely they were. Flying south. The Indians say their path is a pattern in the stars. Maybe so." She held the coat tight against herself. "But the wind. There's more to the wind than listening, Aunt Beatrice. When ducks fly south, they hold the wind in its course."

She paused and turned the knob in her hand, noiselessly back and forth.

"One drake, two hens."

* * * * *

Any plan I might have entertained for intervening further in the situation was far less clear than my decision to do so. Thus, my visits to Minneapolis following Maria's death while infrequent, had only one purpose. Joanna had become my deepest concern. Events, if they alone did not fully determine my purpose, certainly shaped it, set it in direct opposition to the assumption Fritz held that he had any real claim to control over her.

What he had overlooked, and what he soon found himself unable to cope with in her was what lay far less gracefully within himself: an unbending will to do as he saw fit, and an equal rectitude respecting its fitness. Particularly, as in her it also harbored a streak of her mother's seemingly unaccountable waywardness, yet was balanced by a sensitivity that I regarded as uniquely Joanna's, and a sagacity absent in Fritz.

It was hardly remarkable that the distance between the two of them became unbridgeable following Maria's death. Left with the only choice that remained to him, Fritz spent nearly all of his time in Chicago, leaving Joanna alone with the servants in the house. Her protective acceptance of that abandonment may have been mutable, but Joanna had made it complete to her needs. It was a separation that seemed not to disturb her. It was a relief, rather. Her acceptance of a necessary and satisfactory turning point.

She seemed quite aware that she could have no real control of her own future for another year and a half when she would be eighteen. Seeing little need to do more than rest quietly within herself, patiently confident of the freedom she would command, watchful, waiting, and increasingly self assured. I don't expect she was surprised when Fritz returned that final fall for the expressed purpose of going duck hunting. Nor was there any doubt that she would have refused to join him had he asked. Certainly to avoid him, but just as certainly for a reason of her own that was revealed to me after the fact, she had chosen to be away from home until Fritz left for Deerwood.

Joanna already knew far more about her mother than I realized. Matters in Maria's life that it perhaps would have been better that she learned of at some later time had it been my opportunity to control their revelation. For what had been a temporary and heedless adventure, not overburdened with either sensitivity or sincerity, and tarnished with fear, was a disposition natural, vital and honest in her daughter.

The week her father was in Deerwood, Joanna had spent with a schoolgirl friend. They were enjoying what was by then a year-long, fully realized love affair; mutually agreeable, clear and unquestioned. And which, she made no particular effort to conceal.

For all that time, she had the house to herself. What responsibility the servants had been charged with seemed not to have involved her personal behavior. If it had, she would have considered it invasive and ignored it. She was free, within her own constraints, to do as she chose. And she did. Neither her choice, nor her expression of it was mine to judge. It was her want of prudence I felt obliged to call to her attention. And to do so in a manner the transparency of which would not be lost to her.

* * * * *

Joanna was standing with her back to the fireplace, gazing at nothing in particular, a look of troubled preoccupation on her face. That she was thinking about the inquest or its outcome would seem to have been less than central to her thoughts.

"Are you cold?" I asked.

"What? No, I'm sorry, Aunt Beatrice. Habit, I guess." She smiled a little and then sat opposite me in the wing chair by the fire. The chair that had always seemed a shelter for her against the exposures so common in that room.

"You know what the situation is, Joanna. You will have to come up to Duluth with me now. Something I'm sure is not distasteful to you."

"Of course not. It's being ordered to do it that I don't like. You know that."

"That's an order over which we have some control. For a while, at least."

"Enough so I can stay here and finish school? I've got to finish twelfth here, Aunt Beatrice. Then I guess I can enroll at Duluth fall quarter."

"You're through here in the spring."

"I can come up in the summer."

"Perhaps."

"What does perhaps mean?"

"That, Joanna, is up to you. For the moment, your responsibilities are mine. Between us, they are yours. I don't expect you to forfeit them. For any reason."

"I'm not going to do that, Aunt Beatrice." Leaning forward in the chair, her elbows on her knees, she raised a hand to run her fingers through her hair above her left ear, a gesture adapted from Fritz long ago. "But I would rather wait until summer. It's important to me."

"I can appreciate that."

"You're forcing me to invent reasons."

"I'm aware that your reason has little to do with invention. And that it will be less important in the spring."

"Perhaps."

"You know, Joanna, I neither enjoy nor find much justice in verbal fencing, whether it's used for advantage or revelation. It seems to me that such encounters usually close the door to the candor I would like to encourage. Especially from you."

"Then there is no point in inventing anything." She got up from the chair and walked to the fireplace and stood with her hands in her pockets, her back to the fire. "Is there?" And she watched me carefully with the same intense blue gaze, the same command of gesture and the brief silence it defined; she appropriated the moment just as she had in the train station two years before. But this time with deliberation.

"I saw her father's letter to you, Aunt Beatrice. Yesterday, on the hall table. On his office letterhead." She ran her hand through her hair again and smiled suddenly, wry and disbelieving. "God. I suppose he dictated it to his secretary."

"Apparently. I thought that a rather tactless

approach, too. However, distance is a necessary comfort for him, I expect. He will be accommodated."

"You're going to answer it?"

"Yes. Through my attorney."

"I'm not asking you to understand." She had hesitated before she spoke.

"That's not necessary."

"That you understand?"

"For you to ask that."

"Why not?"

"Because I do. Far more than you realize."

I had sought candor. If that challenged her, she met it. If that invited her own, I had willingly risked it.

"You're remarkably steady under fire, aren't you?" I said. "But for you to be otherwise would really disappoint me."

"Aunt Beatrice, why are you making this so easy for me?" And she looked at me suddenly. With doubt, recognition, embarrassment and relief. A small, condensed shock of realization.

"You and I will have much to talk about, Joanna. When summer comes."

I suppose it satisfies a pernicious need in those who are otherwise well-meaning, to not only seek causes for behavior deemed inadmissable, but to accept only those that promise the possibility of control over it. Causes insisting that Fritz shaped Joanna thus, or that Maria's weaknesses left her daughter unformed and bereft of a mother after whom she would have more acceptably patterned herself. Through years of oppressive attention and the unintended mercy of significant neglect, Joanna was drawing on a sense of herself that lay deeper within her than mere suggestion could reach. Joanna was, simply, given.

And if she has been given to me through a series of events it is useless to any longer ponder, I cannot say that I am not gratified. I feel quite justified now in guiding and protecting her. However much I may feel compelled to exact intelligence and grace and the acquisition of prudence, she will be rewarded by their uses. For Joanna at least, there will be no denials.

The View From An
Oriel Window

I don't remember when I first saw Joanna Becker. But I do know that by both fortune and design I was made fatefully aware of her one early April day in 1949. A day when the sun with spring's first reminder of a sentience within had released Duluth from winter. Bathed then in that restless renewal, a sudden need to emerge from the frozen cave of one's self blinds the mind for a moment and the eyes search for lilacs and loveliness to possess. Mine found Joanna.

She had that clear ethereal assurance, birthright of innocence given carelessly to young boys poised on the equivocal brink of a manhood that for them will blur and finally corrode it forever, and that goes so perversely unobserved in young girls. Joanna will keep it; a simple natural gain to a uniqueness that was to be amiably enriched that summer with a bounty touched with feral grace and yet malleable to refined containment. It all added to her beauty, sobered her thoroughly dazzling countenance, but otherwise changed her little. Joanna will remain one of those rarified perfections among us who, ages on, wither imperceptibly, dry defiantly and seem ultimately to drift off as dust drifts on the gold of quiet melancholy afternoons.

I like to fall in love. Maybe this has something to do with a remote Teutonic inheritance seasonally robust in me that I betray by a happy awareness of its theatrical and comforting doom. Wandering from the previous summer among ancestral European landscapes to the winter bleakness of the university at Duluth seemed an astringent, corrective choice. It was also closer to home and the indulgent support of my remarkable mother.

Actually, my beggared inheritance is more closely related to that one summer's wishful languor than to any verifiable genetic support, my father being Swiss of mostly French background and my mother distinctly Parisienne. But it was a pleasant fancy and its very frailty had something to do with finding Joanna so attractive.

She had legitimate claim to a deep-running and less spurious chord to account for her outward glacial aloofness, resonant as it was with an air of bleak sadness and remote loss. Yet it was difficult not to suspect some pose in her whole stance because it was so completely opposed to the most guileless, the most exquisite sensuality I had yet known. Or ever would again, I feared. Then it was the most tangible thing about her, and filled our summer with the jeweled distance from care and consequence that shapes the one sense of self that fortifies forever against all that falsifies the rest of our lives.

I had walked across the Common from the Hall of Music, open-throated to the spring, rejoicing in a wave of yellow crocus awakened from their bed of snow, dreaming of lilacs when I saw her standing alone, aslant from her own shadow as it shortened toward noon. She was hatless and golden in the sun, wearing the traditional red and black check mackinaw of college students and North Shore fishermen. The usual short boots, the usual wool trousers, the usual books under her arm. What was unusual was the directness of her gaze and the invitation in her stance.

It is pointless to wander even the smallest part of the world in pursuit of fantasy and then scorn its arrival. She gazed at me for one more confident moment, shifted her books from one hip to the other and said with an admirable simplicity and calm, "You've been watching me for days. It's time to know why."

"I'm sure you do."

"Yes. But this is no place to be talking about it."

That is how it came about that I went for the first time to her Great Aunt Beatrice's house.

Duluth then was still an old city, its tacky World War Two façade already beginning to collapse against the backdrop of a nineteenth century beginning, imperious in its command of the steep harbor-side hills, its destiny to monopolize the great open pits of its mined affluence, its unlimited view of the heroic industriousness of the harbor and the appropriated waters of Lake Superior that filled the whole horizon.

Great Aunt Beatrice's house stood like an elaborate finial at the utmost reach of a street driving to the top of the steepest of those hills. The Mesabi earth and all the treasure it held had belonged without question to her people. If their assumptive destiny held that others of their resourceful faith would transform the forests of Wisconsin beyond the south shore of that vast lake to the yielding meadows of today, then hers would scour the limitless red iron from the earth of Minnesota and send it forth down the length of the lake to transform it into gold. Great Aunt Beatrice Fröeling was what remained of one of those families of great-hearted plunderers. The gold had built that iron house of American Gothic certitude into whose sequestered clasp she had, with a determined confidence, given Joanna the year before. Standing against the clear April sky, its tall clustered chimneys exceeding the command of the hill, portico flanked by stern bowed windows, it appeared a house of austerely judgmental welcome.

Joanna had driven us to the top of the street in

a hoarsely grinding army surplus Jeep, snow tires holding us in the alpine ascent of some mad arctic bat on a blind course to its gothic aerie. And in the sudden visceral drop to flat ground as she raced the Jeep through the long drive and under the front portico, I caught a glimpse of a lovely little oriel window in the small room that extended above, radiant in the bright noon sun. The little window, as I discovered, let out upon the most beautiful view of the lake from anywhere in the house. But that room's greatest treasure was the view it revealed to me of Joanna.

We sat for a moment wrapped in the quick warmth stillness brings when a drive against the wind ceases. Joanna turned and smiled at me and then gathered up my books from the floor of the Jeep and handed them to me, and after picking up her own stepped out into the snow and stood waiting for me to follow.

"Coming?"

"Yes, of course." I may have been watching, but she had quite obviously been preparing for this.

"You're about to meet my Great Aunt Beatrice."

"LeBrecque. That's my last name, I mean. Victoria LeBrecque."

"I know."

"And you're sure she will approve, too."

"Without a doubt."

And I followed her through the open bench-lined portico into a house whose iron began perceptibly to melt. I had misjudged it. Embellished with elaborate carved verge boards and great gables, its rural air must have been considered quaint at one time but now it had a kind of strong, independent and accommodating comfort. A wide, easy vestibule gave into an embracing hall waist-high with the sheen of oak rubbed by a devoted hand, a rich Persian runner on the floor deepened the soft rose painted walls. Along the way to the left was a small library where Joanna paused for a moment, her hand on the doorjamb, looking as though she were about to say something. Across from it, the dining room where through an opposite doorway I could just see what I soon discovered was the parlor.

Gazing, I must have lingered, savoring some greater expectation, yet unwilling to squander the mounting warmth of that passage, when I looked up to see Joanna standing at the center of a greater transverse open hall in a light of intense rose, on a carpet of richer colors that seemed to shift and waver, moving with the sunlight, repeating and swelling and spreading the floating stained glass pattern of four magnificent doors leading to the veranda and the gardens beyond. She stood slowly taking off her coat and then she helped me off with mine with the same quiet smile, the same deliberation, and hung them both on great polished wooden pegs under the staircase going up at the end of the hallway. She stacked our books on a bench beneath them. All the while her presence was wrapped, it seemed, around me, but her attention was clearly elsewhere. She was looking for Aunt Beatrice.

"She's in the parlor." And we turned from that lovely hallway, beyond draperies sashed firmly aside from the veranda doors, and went on into Aunt Beatrice's great bow-windowed parlor, its arched-work ceiling mixed in some miraculous way with oak and a blacker wood, the lighted fireplace glowing opposite the windows. Beside the fireplace on one of two full velvet settees sat a handsome woman of unquestioned dignity; self-possessed, calm and with a quiet almost wry smile that betrayed the severity of dark, silvered hair drawn up in a chic French roll. It was a smile with which I was already familiar, not yet uneasy about.

Joanna bent to kiss her Great Aunt's cheek and in the same movement turned toward me and said, "This is Vicki, Aunt Beatrice."

That introduction lacking somewhat the grace of the kiss, Aunt Beatrice paused to turn a ring on her hand and then looked at me with just the proper mixture of apology and appraisal. "You will forgive Joanna, I expect. She is given to announcing things full blown. Since I find I seldom disagree with her, however ill-prepared she leaves me, I'm delighted she's brought you here at last, Victoria."

Ordinarily, even at that time in my life, I had no great difficulty in attaching, if not always correctly defining, motive to remarks like that. Neither the moment nor the remark was ordinary, no more ordinary than the whole lovely intense rose aura that my bemused smile must surely have reflected.

Aunt Beatrice glanced at Joanna who stood respectfully with her back to the fire, as if in attendance upon some necessary ritual, but apparently despairing of any response from either of us. "She spoke of you at breakfast last week, Victoria. Which of course was her way of acquainting me with a situation I presume is of some standing."

I had already made the commitment Joanna was waiting for. "Yes, some. But I'm sure it will be greater."

"Then I expect you will be staying with us. Joanna is pleased, therefore, I'm sure I am."

What Joanna had announced, to use Aunt Beatrice's word, was clear; what she had meant it to convey to me was obvious and so singularly lacking in overture that I was a little stunned. What I had thought to be a delightfully deliberate and hardly unusual pursuit on my own part had become forthright appropriation on hers, adorned with an abrupt honesty and an unquestioned self-possession utterly new to me, utterly disarming. It simply had not occurred to me that she had, in her way, been pursuing me. It was to be the only time I would underestimate Joanna Becker.

By mid-week, I was putting my clothes and books and whatever else I had with me at school into two ancient dufflebags that constituted my luggage. That meant leaving my room vacant unless I found someone disorganized enough for the balance of the spring term to need it. The two women who shared next to me seemed to yell at one another often enough to offer a promise of picking up the balance of my fee.

Folding shirts and skirts and jeans and my one obligatory dress, socks and my underclothes and pajamas, I moved in the detachment of all of yesterdays' rose-hued afternoons. The fragrance, the savor of satiate nights invested my mind, perhaps my reason, most certainly my whole being with a flood of remembered rhythms and the mutuality of sensation possible only when likeness is both unity and identity. We had slept, Joanna and I, clasped as the counters of the grain of the wood of one tree.

I stood at the window looking out upon the same great bank of yellow crocus, dazzling in the spring sun, the snow melting away in the gentlest of rivulets, loosening the soft brown earth away from stems vestal green above the spreading leaves.

Pushing the last of my books and my small alarm clock into the duffles, I sat at the empty desk and wrote a note to leave next door. That act recalled me to the practicalities at hand, and at the bottom of the note I added my post box number in the Music Department. Joanna had left the Jeep for me in front of the dormitory and gone on with Aunt Beatrice attending to whatever errands their mute ordained signals had arranged during dinner the night before.

My joy, my desire, my need for Joanna was unburdened by any question. I gathered up my two dufflebags, locked the door behind me, pushed the note under the door up the hall and almost ran down the stairs. I found the keys under the seat of the Jeep, imagined them still warm from her hand, made a joyous U-turn and headed for Aunt Beatrice's house to renew the embrace of the little room with the oriel window.

The Jeep ground and complained under my inexpert command, the improvised cushions warding off some of the shocks of its jolting gait. One learned to roll a bit with it, giving in finally, like complying to the unbending stubbornness of a horse of uncertain breed. Resigned to that, I found myself thinking about Aunt Beatrice's piano. I suppose the discovery of it had been so delightful because, in the

rare sane moments of the preceding three days, I
could, if I had to, account for the decision I was now
carrying out by arguing that I would no longer have
to confine practice time to the availability of a piano
in the Music Building.

Just how it had gotten up to the great
bow-windowed room above the parlor with its deep
fireplace and fine double windows overlooking the
side garden seemed one more entrancing puzzle. I
speculated that the house could have been built
around it, but it being obvious that the piano was
rather newer, I accepted Joanna's explanation. Aunt
Beatrice had arranged for the temporary removal of
the windows, a space quite ample for a grand piano
to pass through. Did she still use it? Yes,
occasionally, but not as often as in the past and it
was mine to use now. It was finer than any at
school, quite in keeping with everything else in the
house.

Nowhere was there an abandoned or insentient
spot. No room without its air of expectancy, or a
sense of someone richly alive having just touched
some book or exquisitely decorated box or sculptured
bird, turned up a lamp, drawn aside a drapery;
about to return. The piano bench seemed often
pushed back in pleasant interruption, the sound of
the music just stilled in the rooms.

Abiding in the devoted care of two servants, Aunt
Beatrice and Joanna filled the house. Clara cooked
and her husband Carl helped her clean, laid fires in
the endless fireplaces, looked after the small gardens
nearest the house, and chauffeured, both of them
seeming always to be providing countless other small
amenities as well.

Beyond the upstairs music room to the rear was another master bedroom, above Aunt Beatrice's. Silent in the quiet light of afternoons, with its daily bowl of fresh flowers that, since they were everywhere else in the house would have been more noticeable had they been absent, it seemed always to be a room empty of everything but a significance lost to me then. But it was the suite of three rooms off the transverse upstairs hallway with its stained glass windows perhaps less elaborate than the doors to the veranda below, that Joanna had chosen for her own. A bedroom with a small bath at the far west side of the house, and a larger sitting room she used as a study with a great mullioned window at the front.

Between these two rooms and accessible only through them was the small room with the oriel window, extending out over the portico. That small room was the only room in the house without a fireplace, but it hardly needed it. The seat inside the window was cushioned in brocades and velvets and watered silks. A wide and handsome couch of some obscure and immoderate design luxuriated in a quilted silk throw in the colors of a hundred impossible gardens, a Bokhara rug of indescribable beauty covered most of the waxed wood floor. Rubbed oak embraced the walls breast high. One lamp's light of warm and modest suggestion held the night in balance each time it came.

That room was a lotused sanctuary, a sybaritic climax of all the other loveliness and charm of the house that surrounded it. I was made more drunken each time I entered it. And it was there that Joanna's pose of a being bleak and sadly wronged was abandoned. It wasn't that she had not been wronged, and rather sadly at that as I soon found, but she had exacted from that experience a useful, defensive coloration. Behind it she shielded the vulnerability of an outright, unabashed, intuitively perfect sensuality. She was utterly knowing and exquisitely gifted with delicacy, exuberance, and a generosity that never once strained the uncountable threads that tied our emotions and the embracing delights our bodies shared. Self-possessed at seventeen, serene in her intelligence, she simply knew all it had taken me a longer, sometimes anguished, albeit gently tutored time to learn.

The Jeep labored up the last agonizing pitch of the climb to the top of the hill and flung itself onto the flat curving drive to Aunt Beatrice's house. Up there the snow lay crusted and sparkling in the sun, the thaw seeping away from beneath and out onto the drive. I slowed down, aware that I had paid little attention to all the carefully nurtured naturalness that sheltered the approach to the house and led so pleasantly up the drive. The shadbush still looked ragged and spare at the turn, but lovely clusters of elm and hemlock were already swelling with the mauve haze of spring and the maples flashed blunt red buds against the black branches of the oaks that would shade the house in the heedless summer to come.

Under the portico I gazed straight ahead through some last-century landscaper's skillfully selected stand of white paper birch left so tight at points as to now prohibit passage, then thinned discreetly to lead the eye and tempt trespass down indeterminate paths. Until through the chattering idle of the Jeep's engine I heard the thick sound of a gun being fired into the wall of the humid spring air.

One shot, then two quickly together. A pause and then the pattern repeated twice, three times. Some fragment of conversation, some small, taught reference, a quickly passing ripple in an otherwise agreeable conversation at dinner with Aunt Beatrice the night before reawakened without any particular alarm in my mind. I shifted down and drove on through the portico, around the west side of the house past the kitchen chimneys and on to the old stable. The shots continued in their methodical pattern. Aunt Beatrice's car was inside the stable door. Looking back, I saw the smoke rising straight up from the chimney cluster above the parlor. She was there, of course.

I don't like guns. They have entered the shadows of my life in ways remote from the rich suggestion of sporting arms. I ground the gears a bit and jolted past the dormant kitchen garden and out through the rows of bare fruit trees into the open field and stopped.

Joanna was there alone, standing in a kind of odd called-up attention, a tan sleeveless hunting vest over the heavy bright red shirt she had been wearing when she dropped me at school in the morning. As I watched, she moved one foot toward the trap stand at her elbow and in the same concentrated motion raised the long thin black shotgun she held in her hands. The two clay birds spun out and crossed against the sky and she brought the gun to her shoulder and swung gun and body and being to the left and then to the right in the same pattern and two sharp reports shattered

the clay in two explosive bursts. The fragments spun
and drifted away in the air, the undulating echo
swelled and then lay still inside of me.

Joanna reloaded the gun with bright yellow
shells, and I stepped from the Jeep and walked
down the footsteps she had made in the wet snow.

"Hello. I didn't know you were so good at that."

"You saw the good shots."

"I don't believe that. How do they fly?"

"The levers down there. One for one, two for two.
I just step on them."

"Which one?"

"Whichever you like. I'll hear them."

I stepped on two first and she hit them both.
Within a second or so it seemed, she had reloaded
the gun and I sent one more clay bird out which
she also hit and without looking at me she said,
again, and broke the gun open. The shell she held
between the fingers of her left hand was in the
chamber and the gun at her shoulder again as I
stepped on two in what I had assumed to be my
confusion, and both of those blew apart and drifted
off as I had watched the others do.

Joanna broke the gun open again, releasing the
empty shells, and held it broken open in the crook
of her arm. I moved away from the trap stand and
in the sudden stillness the smell of the powder lay
on the air like some vaguely ominous incense. I
wasn't exactly sure what I felt. That she had a
remarkable and, I supposed by some evaluation,
enviable ability seemed difficult to deny. She was a
formidable and nearly unerring shot with that gun.
Wing shooter, I subsequently learned.

But it was Joanna's other talents, less disturbing

to me, that had quite absorbed my attention and had only begun to satisfy my expectations of her. Because of that I guessed it would have been less than wise not to comment on this performance. She smiled at me as though she were somehow trying to emerge from some hard, separate and studiously defined image of herself.

"Want to try it?"

"No. I guess not."

And for a fleeting moment she retreated, as she had on the first day in the rose hallway, still defining the quality of our space, but focused on some other part of herself and then just as quickly returned. "Aunt Beatrice doesn't really like it either."

She was standing with the gun still held in the crook of her arm looking at me with an expression quite unrelated to what she was saying; quite explicitly concentrated on me. "It's been a long time since this morning. I'd like to make up for missing you."

Going back to the Jeep, I walked in the same path of footprints, Joanna beside me making a new set. "I didn't know you were so horribly out-doorsy. I'm getting cold and my nose is running." And besides, I had cramps and a sad sense of dismay about that.

She shifted the gun to her right arm and from a pocket offered a folded piece of Kleenex and while I wiped my nose in a gentler annoyance, she ran her hand up my back holding it warm against the back of my neck while we walked. It was the first time she had touched me outside the shelter of her rooms upstairs.

She snapped the gun shut and stood it upright in

a clamp inside the back of the Jeep close to my two dufflebags. We got in and she drove back to the kitchen entrance, remarking along the way that I didn't seem to have brought much stuff to school with me and then, ducking her head a little to look into my face, that she would draw me a hot tub right away.

While the water steamed into a tub poised on small porcelained lion feet like some anticipating votive basin, Joanna helped put my things away in an armoire in her bedroom. She did this with what I felt was a nicely revealing sense of appropriate order for the entire process and over which I allowed myself some very satisfied pleasure.

"I can't quite get over having been so confidently planned for."

"I'm a very logical person. Among other things."

"It's the other things, I guess."

"That you like."

"Things like now, yes. That I love very much."

I put my toothbrushes and toothpaste in the bathroom beside hers and spent a doubtful moment wondering what to do with everything else rolled up in my toilet case, discovering at the same time and with despair what I was utterly out of. Joanna was leaning against the doorframe watching my dismay and with a prescience of considerable nicety said, "In the chest over there on the bottom."

"Thank you. How did you know?"

"That glassy look in your eyes, I guess."

I rolled up the case and put it in the bottom of the chest, taking a tampon from the box.

"God, how stupid."

Joanna didn't often smile broadly with that

unique release of feeling for either the joys or the absurdities of life, but she did then. "I don't think being a woman is stupid. If you weren't, that would be the stupidest thing I could think of." And she moved past me to the tub and sat on the edge with her back to me, testing the water, mixing more hot into it with considerable deliberation.

"Come on, I'll scrub your back."

I stretched in the lovely warmth of the water like a lizard in the sun while she sat on the edge of the tub caressing every willing inch I possessed with the look in her eyes, the curve of her mouth. Then she gathered up a big white towel and leaned over with a wry, amused kiss that banked the fire.

"You surprise me," she said. "I thought you listened more carefully."

"To what?"

"To your insides. Just do what they tell you."

"How did you arrive at that?"

"I read a lot."

That evening after dinner, comfortable, relieved and happy, I sipped a brandy, my stockinged feet tucked warm under me on the velvet settee. Gazing into the fire, knowing Joanna was watching every change of expression I might reveal, listening within my luxurious distance to her murmured response to Aunt Beatrice, I was already slipping into the simple bliss of sleeping against the length of her all the night long.

Somewhere at some point in my reverie the small shift of tone in Aunt Beatrice's voice, the gentle appropriating authority grew just a bit brighter than the fire. She was sitting directly opposite on the other settee, with Joanna lounging beside her in the corner, legs stretched out, ankles crossed. The sound of her brandy glass being set on the table, the thin decisive rasp as it was moved away from the edge, counterpoint to the soft flickering of the last of the fire.

"You should ask Victoria how she feels about it, dear. I'm sure it's a decision for both of you."

"I think Vicki is sleepy."

"No, of course not," I said. "I'm sorry. What are we deciding about?"

"I have to go down to Minneapolis at term's end. About the house."

"What about the house?"

"Victoria, I would like you to go with Joanna. There are a few small details to attend to that will settle things. There's no real need for me to be there since her father's attorneys have everything in order. Later, when it will be appropriate, all of this will be placed with our own people." She glanced quickly at Joanna as though she expected this unusual and unguarded reference to her father to have been disturbing. Joanna just continued to look at me without changing her expression. "But as it is now, I'd rather she didn't go alone."

Her thin graceful hand fingered the long strand of pearls, pausing briefly at the knot that tied them. There seemed so little doubt in her mind that the matter was settled, I wondered at that earlier solicitude for my feelings. But it was a wonder slowly beginning to fade, for I had begun to realize that the deliberations weaving me into the fabric of Joanna's peculiarly sheltered life were as binding as they were generous. But within it lay pure license. And it was irresistible.

"That's fine," I said. "It's time for me to see my mother. And for Joanna to."

The last was a simple gamble. And like most gambles, the odds lay in that realm of indifferent resignation so regretlessly left to spirits then more acute than mine.

"That might well be wise," Aunt Beatrice said.

Quite careless of where that wisdom may have lain, I looked to Joanna to be met again with the same quiet smile, and I surrendered to it. My mood then would not admit to delving further into Aunt Beatrice's motives. And when she added with an air of almost innocent amusement, "I think Victoria is sleepy, Joanna. Perhaps you should tuck her into bed," I barely caught the innuendo.

All the succeeding days dawned clear blue and golden and we watched the crusted snows melt away. With summer promised we lost ourselves to each other in the lavish sanctuary of Aunt Beatrice's ordered, rose-hued house. We were free within it, undisturbed by her unspoken demand for decorum outside of it. I buried myself satisfied and undistracted in yet another semester of harmony and counterpoint, practiced all the requisite hours each day at Aunt Beatrice's great Baldwin upstairs with a willingness and at a level of progress and success that both pleased and surprised me, and which I felt might lend hope to my mother's conviction that somewhere manifest in my "reliable ear and quick and accurate mind" lay her imprint, the mark of a serious musician.

After classes, Joanna worked in the study by the ever-present fire, or infrequently she would be gone for long stretches on what I assumed was business

with Aunt Beatrice. The Jeep carried us faithfully
down and back up that incredible hill from school
each necessary day and we measured the splendor of
the new green forest sequestering the house more
and more until the end of May and summer enclosed
us. By night we lay in the flowered silk couch while
the moon shone naked through the oriel window.

One afternoon as the semester dwindled down,
after almost five hours of grim practice, I gave up
and walked wearily into the study to find Joanna
working at the desk surrounded by a stack of books
and briefs and sheafs of paper memoranda. The fire
lay in embers behind the screen and she looked up
at me with that familiar bleakness I had almost
gotten used to.

"I didn't know you were here," I said. "I hope all
that didn't disturb you."

"No." And she smiled and added, "You play a lot
better than Aunt Beatrice." She finished writing
some notes and while she was still looking at what
she had written she said, "You've never really told
me what you think about my studying this stuff."

"No, I guess I haven't." And I hadn't. Joanna had
enrolled herself as a law major and the first time
she talked about it the most important thing she
had said was that she was doing it because she
didn't like the law. She wanted to change it. At
least some parts of it. It was a conversation easily
picked up. "But I guess I don't like some of it
either, so I see your point. But changing it is going
to take a lot of doing, I'd think."

She leaned back in her chair with a pencil

clenched across her teeth for a moment and then she grinned at me. "Well, if I could have majored in overthrowing the government I would have, but it's not offered."

"You're the most mercurial idiot I ever knew."

"You know something, Vicki. The law says my father was killed accidentally. That's a lot of crap. He killed himself."

"Maybe. Maybe not."

"No. That's it. He killed himself."

"Why?"

"Because he couldn't think of what else to do. Because he followed all the rules he believed in and made a mess of everything. Of Mother, a botch of me. End of the line."

"I hardly think you're a botch."

"He did. I suppose he even bought the monster myth." She gathered up the notes she had been working on and jogged them together into a neat square stack beside the books. "There's something else, too. My mother died because she drank herself to death and the law called that natural causes. And that's not quite true either because he drove her to it. He wanted her dead. I don't think that's a natural cause. At least not for her."

That was the most she had ever yet said to me about her parents and she was saying it with a detachment that told me a great deal more than the small allusions that had come up on occasion in our conversations with Aunt Beatrice and which I felt uncomfortable about pursuing. I had not quite wanted to defrock Joanna of the outward air of penance and pain she wore so protectively outside the shelter of the house. Now, with clarity, she had made that move quite unnecessary.

"Sometimes," I said, "I do wonder how come you're so smart."

"Necessity. I don't want to be one of those people who wake up at forty-five and say, if I'd only known then what I know now. By then I hope I'll be inventing what nobody knows yet."

Maybe living with Aunt Beatrice had stripped Joanna absolutely bare of cant. Or at least the most damaging of illusions. Considering all that had happened to her it wasn't likely that she would waste very much of her life on any.

Two days before Joanna and I were to drive down to Minneapolis, she had one last early class and in the soft haze of that late May morning I walked with her to the Jeep. She stood shaking the keys in her hand for a moment and then she stepped close against me and with one hand on my shoulder she kissed me with a new and surprising mixture of longing and what I would have to say now was an assured, relieved honesty. At the moment it seemed a foolish lack of discretion. That I was startled despite my obvious pleasure apparently delighted her. With a look of amused confidence, she said, "Aunt Beatrice is going to tell you all about it now. Sit tight." And she drove off.

That Aunt Beatrice would have something to say about it seemed unavoidable. My unfinished breakfast, my anticipated second cup of coffee, even the pleasant conversation we had been absorbed in as the three of us sat at the table in the glass enclosed breakfast atrium overlooking the veranda was left ready to be uneasily resumed. From the breakfast table, the Jeep had been in full view.

I went back to Aunt Beatrice to finish my breakfast and not to resume our conversation, but to start quite another. She was pouring herself a cup of coffee as I sat down, and with a grace that in my anxious embarrassment I felt to be a deliberate evasion, she refilled my own cup and suggested fresh hot toast if I would like it.

"No, no need, thank you. It's just fine."

"Victoria, I want you to realize you are in a situation in which you are quite free. As long as you remain in it."

My toast had gotten cold and my concentration on chewing it was doing little more than returning it to a dough in my mouth that threatened to be indigestible. I resorted to the hot coffee, not yet ready to face her, waiting for what could possibly follow such a statement. It struck me as incredible that this woman who appeared to be living so uniquely removed from ordinary reality, yet doing it so charmingly, could possibly go beyond that thought. Seeing her standing there in a simple dark red velvet robe, her long, thin fingers almost as transparent as the china cup she held, I was aware again just how intimidatingly tall she was. I simply did not answer. She gazed for what seemed a very long and silent moment through the windows in the direction Joanna had driven.

"If you think that I am unaware of Joanna's nature, it will be best that I disabuse you. At the same time, I assure you that I am neither surprised nor displeased that she has chosen to express it toward you."

"What can I possibly say?"

"Only what you care to. Joanna has already told me what she felt it necessary to say. That is enough. As for the rest, I regard it as a matter private to the two of you."

I learned that morning that blunt truth is not quite the gratifying release from anxiety or confusion or even guilt we delude ourselves into believing it will be. Only people like Aunt Beatrice ever seem to have that elevated sense of the futility, the utter needlessness for any tactic but the pronouncement of blunt truth. For her, that was a privilege and a gift. She was offering its advantage to me with the obvious suggestion that she felt me possessed of enough wit to move to the level required to accept it.

"If she told you that she is in love with me, then I must tell you that I share that. I love her. I don't know how long this will last. For either of us."

Aunt Beatrice sat down again, placing her cup back into its saucer with gentle deliberation. All that was necessary to make both meaning and conviction utterly clear. "I expect it will last as long as you both wish it to. But I am determined that Joanna will not be hurt by it. Nor by its loss. There is absolutely nothing I can do, nor would ever propose to do to change her. I simply do not believe it either possible or necessary. But I can shelter her, and I mean to. I'm sure you can understand that. She is not that much younger than you, Victoria, but the difference is crucial."

"I know. Yet sometimes she seems so much older. She has very few illusions."

"But the few she has are most precious for now. And that, of course, is my point."

"Forgive me, but I would like to keep a few of my own. They are precious, too."

"Of course. I had depended on that."

Bent on dalliance, idle and close to carelessness, I had fallen in love with someone golden and handsome, with amazing hands, a lean and supple body that fit to me like my own bone and an honest innocence I was not to assume with impunity. Aunt Beatrice's grant was to Joanna; I was quite simply an ingredient of it. Weighed, assessed, approved of, even welcomed; but an ingredient. So, the choice was my own. My obligation was to myself but she had given me to Joanna and Aunt Beatrice gave only what she knew was hers to give.

At all such times there was a tone in Aunt Beatrice's voice that seemed to control the very temperature of the room, the cut of the light, and shape the response she sought. Mine would come as she wanted it, yet somehow retaining just enough of the integrity I thought I had endowed it with to account for my surrender. The difficulty was that Aunt Beatrice was right. Not because her powers of reasoning were superior but because she had created the situation and knew it better than anyone else. The small wry smile returned to her face with, I will admit, a certain modesty.

"I trust you'll not think I've been intemperate, Victoria."

"I guess I'm just amazed by all this."

"I don't think you are. Your own mother would be no less candid, I'm sure."

However she had learned that truth I could no longer wonder at. "In the same circumstances, yes, my mother would be. I guess my father has always loved her enough to leave it up to her." That last gratuitous remark was a fool's regression to just the kind of falsity Aunt Beatrice divined with ease and that deserved a far less gracious response than she gave it.

"I see no reason to excuse his neglect, although that is less harmful than interference."

She paused and looked at me with what seemed a slightly preoccupied air, and then she rose from the table. "Joanna would have far stronger words for that, Victoria. Which I will leave to her."

Very early the next morning I awoke aware that Joanna no longer lay beside me. The sun was just coming up and I felt oddly but not alarmingly deserted. She had not been gone long. The bed was still warm where she had lain, her fragrance just fading along my side.

I turned on my back, bunching the pillows under my head, listening for her in the quiet of the house awakening in its wood to the morning. Through the open windows I watched the crowns of the paper birches begin to glow in the rising sun and followed a tiny nuthatch working her way with concentrated care down one trunk, moving in matching coloration against the piebald bark. As she wound her way around to the other side of the tree intent on her breakfast, I caught the strong and lovely scent of coffee and Joanna returned, bare-footed, wrapped in a short silk robe I had not seen before. Rich and dark with amazing small blue flowers that matched her eyes.

She set the tray she carried with its cups and small pot of steaming coffee on the table beside the bed, smiling at me with her familiar look of innocence and knowing and remembered first nakedness that never failed to kindle mornings into a glow we often fed to flame. Now, the hot coffee, her kiss, her blue flower eyes, her hands along my bare ribs were all pleasure enough.

"Let's go sit in the window and watch the sun come up." And she handed me another short silk robe from the chaise across the room.

"I'm not sure which I like most next to me. One of these or you."

"They were my mother's," she said simply and picked up the tray.

Warm within the oriel window, surrounded by cushions, we watched the sunrise burnish the opalescent lake. The water moved in an expanding rhythm at each touch of the rising breeze, and the flash of the sun measured in fantastic exactitude an infinite pattern of daylit stars across the whole horizon. Joanna seemed intent on watching the lake; sober, uninclined to speak. She had loosened her robe, open deep to her waist, the sun bright on her chest, the dark vertical bars of shadow from the window marking her, bending and then diffusing in the bright blue flowers. I drank the last of my coffee. She set her own empty cup beside mine on the window ledge, and leaning forward she opened my robe with both hands, drew it down off my shoulders.

"It will never fly in Comp 101, but there are bars on both of us, Vicki." And she traced one with a finger across my shoulder, down through the hollow of my throat, moving out to another, tracing it down until her hand closed softly over my breast. "They're going to keep me locked up for a while yet."

"You're forgiven. Maybe I'll like being locked up."

Her hand moved down, warm and still, resting on the small fold against my thigh. "That could be true," she said.

"Do you want it to be?"

"How can I know? Has it been true for you before?"

Whatever was true for Joanna then lay neither in the flat cool blue of her gaze nor the suggestion in her hand. The serenity of her self assurance was doing a little pacing back and forth between uncertainties. This girl I loved was seventeen and looking far beyond, guided by strong instinct and a tempered caution. Candor with Aunt Beatrice was clear and unadorned. Now, reflected in Joanna's question, her touch, the invitation to her body, it was losing all its simple clarity. What had been an easy truth the morning before seemed so no longer.

"Things change. Perhaps I have."

She looked out over the lake for a moment, squinting her eyes against the sun that hid the other shore. "When I know as much about myself as Aunt Beatrice does, maybe I can say that too."

"Well, you do amaze me, knowing things without seeming to have been taught."

"No one is untaught."

"Then there's a lot you haven't told me."

Her fingers spread with an assertive little pressure against the bone of my hip and she tightened her hand over me, her smile breaking into a grin of pleased conviction. "You know perfectly well

Aunt Beatrice didn't put me in this cage just because I was an orphan."

"Sybaritic hot house, I would say. Considering how you've flowered."

"I was already well on my way. Aunt Beatrice is a very cool and practical lady. One step ahead of Mrs. Astor. Just don't frighten the horses."

"You're going to have to forsake this lotus land one day."

"Not until I have my money."

"So you can create another?"

"No. That's another thing I don't like about the world."

"Overthrow it?"

"Just part of it."

Perhaps I was looking particularly credulous at that moment, or maybe it was just that the odd twists to Joanna's sense of disquiet that I'd not got fully used to were eluding me. She leaned over and kissed me and then she laughed and said, "I didn't fall off the turnip truck yesterday, you know."

"God, I guess not. So what is it you haven't told me?"

"Well, for one thing, I made love with a girl I knew in school. Almost all last year. She got scared finally and said she was going to tell her parents. I told her to go ahead if she could figure out how to do it." She paused for a moment and then she added, "She did. And Aunt Beatrice came down to Minneapolis again and told me point-blank that I was going to spend the rest of the year in Duluth developing discretion and better taste, as she put it."

"Your Aunt Beatrice has a very gracious way of dispensing with illusions."

"So far."

"That's a dreadful thing to say. But I am impressed that you put a year to such astonishingly good use."

"That's not dreadful?"

"Yes, but it's also the truth."

"Fair enough. But I really didn't learn anything. Nothing I didn't already seem to know. Except that somehow I wasn't supposed to know it. Or my body didn't have the right to it, or something dumb like that. She was a very beautiful girl. It seemed so idiotic that she could make me explode so beautifully like that. That she could want so much lovely sex with me and enjoy it and still be afraid of where it came from. Some girls, I guess I just don't understand."

The sun had risen higher into the morning, the light framed by the window slanting its firm pattern out across the waxed floor at our feet, across the rug and reaching out to the couch against the wall. Joanna stood up, looking out at the lake again for a moment and then she bent over me drawing the robe up over my shoulders. The blue flowers were back in her eyes and she knew it. She kissed me again. Hard.

"That's not true," she said. "I do understand them. I just don't want to have time for them. Not yet." She looked at me with a sudden and surprised gravity. "I hope you don't ever get tired of being in love with me. You're going to get cold. Come over here."

I was and I hadn't realized it. She drew back the silk comforter and I slid gratefully under it beside her again against her already naked body in the soft protection of the couch.

She held me with one arm around my waist inside the silk robe, the other hand gentle, practiced, connecting and lingering long on the button of my breast; moving down to trace the contour of my thigh. And then she turned the robe aside and moved on top of me, close and tight along my whole spare length. There is no accounting for my offering then a fleeting condolence for the unfortunate girl who gave Joanna up for fear. But the thought came and then quite accountably went, sensibly abandoned to the caress of her tongue along the turn of my ear, a caress that gathered urgent purpose somewhere along the line of my jaw and finally took my mouth in the loveliest of kisses. Kisses experimental, exploring and self-assured, keenly aware of my body's invitation to move her hand down and close it tight around me, holding me yet.

Making love for Joanna was an endlessly renewable art. An unquestioned possibility for shared surprise and gentle inventions, small creations of her hands, her mouth and the force of bone that shaped her body. She moved with the delighted certitude of a stream possessing its flow, yielding up its current to a diverting strength, then penetrating the easy course of its natural direction. Idling in warm eddies to contemplate her course, buoyant in rougher water, she gathered up my own pursuit and her whole body followed the thrust of her tongue inside my mouth, her long blunt fingers slipped into me and the slow contrapuntal rhythm of our bodies chased faster with the current and we came together, held our breaths and rolled together through a crash of wild water and fell on the other side laughing in the silent liquid sunshine.

It's a long drive down to Minneapolis, but it was a bright clear day and aside from some rising water in spots, which is a normal enough part of spring, uneventful. At least the weather was uneventful. As it turned out, I drove most of the way, Joanna slept for a time and I found myself preoccupied with my own thoughts, most of them weaving a pattern of need to talk to my mother. By nightfall that pattern had begun to form in responsive logic to figures Joanna could no longer withhold from its completion.

Somewhere around noon we stopped outside of Saint Cloud to get something to eat at a truck stop Joanna suggested, a place where she and her father sometimes ate when out duck hunting; his idea of slumming as she put it. The food, incidentally, was fine, as it usually is for those with sense enough to rely on the ample forthrightness of German cooking, homemade bread and a bottle of beer.

That practical fortification seemed to wake us both out of ourselves and we talked most of the rest of the way, Joanna taking over the driving when we got to Anoka. We explored the possibilities of transferring from Duluth to the Minneapolis campus. Joanna told me she had graduated from University High just before her delightful indiscretion had prompted Aunt Beatrice to bring her so hastily to Duluth. That meant that before she was seventeen, she already had two years of college credits, which

made for a certain leapfrog entry at Duluth.
Nevertheless, transferring was a matter Joanna felt
to be almost totally dependent upon the arrival of
her eighteenth birthday in March, less than a year
away when she would acquire some of her money in
her own right. And Aunt Beatrice's approval, which
it was obvious to me was really the most important
and likely the deciding factor, Joanna's majority
notwithstanding. Her being securely with me made
things a bit more favorable probably, even to the
extent of making transfer at fall semester not
impossible. Although I think we both knew that it
would take a show of considerable sobering on both
our parts.

But there was something else we both knew then
and as we drove along the river into the city,
Joanna's silences lengthened along with the late
afternoon and the imminence of the house on the
bluffs that I suppose was, after all, justification
enough for the bleak box of protection she had built
around herself for so long. But the box, it was clear,
was beginning to cave in. She simply looked at me
in one long moment of naked silence to acknowledge
that practical conversations are a sham, a seductive
refuge demanding blind zeal to support their flimsy
shelter. By the time she turned the car off the river
road and up the short cedar block drive to the
house, the set of her jaw had returned, the pale
anxiety fading the blue of her eyes. She drove in
through the gates and stopped the car at the back
service door opposite the garages.

"Whatever you do, just don't leave me here,
Vicki."

"I'm not going to leave you anywhere, if I can

help it." And I kissed her hard and quickly and with purpose. I guess I just felt it was my turn to be bold, to tell her it was my turn to make something happen.

"Jesus."

"Well, let's not invoke him."

"Mother of God, then."

"Just plain Mother is better."

That broke it down some at least. She gave me a big tight hug, said yes and we got our luggage out of the car just as one of the servants came out to take it.

"I don't think so," Joanna said. We sat talking after dinner by the fire in the living room, only one lamp lit, the dark deep around us. "I'd find it pretty hard to live here again. Even with you."

"Too bad, it's a lovely place, really."

"Not as lovely as Aunt Beatrice's."

"No, I won't argue that."

"Besides, we don't have to. Mother left me another small house on Lake of The Isles."

"You're full of houses."

"I guess so."

"What are you going to do with this one?"

"Sell it, I suppose. Or whatever Aunt Beatrice wants."

We lay in Joanna's bed, the fire at the other side of the room a silent stream of lazy red coals. The books, the letters and an album of photographs she had unlocked from the drawer of her desk were still with us on one side of the bed. A confessional legacy from her mother.

"Do you think your father knew about her?"

"I'm not sure. He took me away from her. That says he did, probably. She was afraid of him and maybe that does too."

"She was afraid of more than that. People don't drink themselves to death because it feels good."

"No, just better."

Joanna was lying on her back, her hands clasped behind her head. Her deep even breathing, her calm, her small absorbed smile a new and satisfied expression of command over her own judgment, her own assessment of what she had known and seen and had managed to keep herself protectively removed from. I pushed some pillows together to lean on and reached for the photographs and the letters stuck together with them. The whole thing seemed so accountable. Almost ordinary. What seemed crazy was that I should have been surprised by it; that a girl like Maria Fröeling could have had an experience like that in her life and then buried it in an imposition of remorse and guilt, and fear for its exposure.

Beautiful, fragile, intensely feminine, resting her head in a revelation of need on the shoulder of a handsome dark-haired woman of obvious strength and firm assertive possession, Maria fixed her gaze on the camera's eye and consigned the only honest passion of her life to a neutral moment in time. I pulled the picture out of its black corners and turned it over. There were four lines written in

French about the foolishness of forgetting in the
same vertical hand as the letters, signed only with
initials and a date, 1924.

"Wouldn't you like to know who D. H. was?"

"Maybe she still is."

"Alive? Would you be afraid of that?"

"No, I don't think so. But I would be jealous of
her."

Joanna pulled herself up and began to search
around in the bed for her pajamas, put the jacket on
and sat with her knees drawn up, her hands clasped
around her ankles. Her remark was innocuous
enough, but the thought that began to form in my
mind was shaped by the tone in her voice and an
unmistakable conviction that her sense of herself was
fixed, clear, and beyond question. She took the
picture out of my hand and after looking at it for a
while set it down in front of her feet.

"I guess it won't surprise you too much, but it's
time to tell you the rest about my mother. And
about me. About what I've just begun to
understand."

She wrapped her arms around her knees and sat
quietly for a moment and then her smile settled into
a gentle sigh. "Would it sound crazy to say that I
fell in love with her? About a year before she died. I
thought I was going crazy. But she was so lovely —
clear and fragile as crystal. Crystal that holds only
itself." She turned a small tuft of wool from the
blanket in her fingers and then she tossed it away.
"She was my mother until I was six or seven or so.
That was when my father got into image-making.
Mine and hers. I never really knew her after that.

After that she wasn't my mother. She was so utterly separated from me. As far as my father was concerned, she had become a totally contemptible woman, and I was supposed to feel as he did. Obviously I didn't. I just didn't feel anything. Until that year."

"Did you tell her?"

"God, I suppose I tried. But I didn't have to. She knew what was happening. I think if she hadn't known she was dying it would have terrified her. Or at least she would have handled it differently. Instead, one afternoon when I had been reading to her, she asked me to sit beside her on the bed and she kissed me. I had never been kissed like that. I found out that day what it means to know a woman's mouth, a woman's kiss. To know my own. I used to think we were both a little mad at the moment. Something seemed to happen to all the prescribed identities. Our returning to each other like that was really the sanest moment either of us had in this house."

The most startling thing about that statement was the expression on Joanna's face. A magic of tenderness and gentle pleasure, of pain and loss and resignation and a terrible need to disbelieve that knowing this was something that had one day to be relinquished. Sensible to having said a simple, honest thing and revealed a nearly unknowable and unspeakable truth. And I know now how aware she was that though it would slip away to lay unformed again in some disordered temporary time to come, she would never really be left without its strength. Knowing it had shaped her. Possessing it would define her for the rest of her life and transcend all other definitions.

I lay awake for a long time with Joanna's head burrowed into my shoulder, the lengthening rhythm of her breathing bearing her pain out along the strength in her body to dissipate for a while like sound that rides away on the wind.

I can't say that I have ever experienced any deprivation in my life. Particularly while I was growing up. Some fear, a lot of disorder, often; periods of transience were fashioned to be a part of my existence before I was born. My mother is a concert pianist. She also teaches. My father plays the violin. That often meant following a regular concert circuit around Europe. Although we moved around a lot, I traveled most often with my mother or when she was teaching, remained with her in a small house on the Rue de La Huchette in Paris. Except when my father toured Italy, or Germany which now holds a particular fascination made up of equal parts horror, sorrow and a deliberate nostalgic blindness.

In the spring of 1939, when I was eleven years old, we fled to the United States. After nearly a year of blissful school-less days wandering around New York, while my mother battled with the United States Immigration Services ultimately establishing us as refugees in this country and my father worked his way west to join the Minneapolis Symphony, things settled down. With the aid of the professional network, my mother put her concert career back

together, was established as a teacher, purchased a
home, and one more dislocated family sequestered
itself in the unworldly remoteness of middle-west
America. While I'm sure we felt this would be for
the duration of the war, in the process we became
Americans, however different from those that
produced Joanna Becker.

Thus while the easy, assumptive affluence which
she had obviously enjoyed all her life, distinct as I
found, from sudden wealth generated by that war at
least, was not fully my lot, the social attributes
upheld and fortified by it are the intellectual
imperative, if not the inherited privilege, of a child
of the *haute bourgeoisie*. I think I was just surprised
to see it in this country. A lot of Europeans then
still held strained Jamesian notions of Americans,
and while people like Great Aunt Beatrice may have
substantiated many such beliefs and, when I dwelt
on it, I may have felt that people like Joanna's
parents came rather closer to some sort of Scott
Fitzgerald vaguery, Joanna to my great delight
defied any such labels. She would supply her own.
That she was a very well-off American wasn't going
to alter that fact. It would for her simply make it
easier and, I felt quite sure, lend considerable grace
to her unruffled honesty.

Yet I was less sure that somewhere in the
inequity of our positions there didn't lay problems
pressing uncomfortably on my own self-assurance.
My view of our situation was lengthening. I needed
some distance if only for a short while. I needed
some direction. Which way Joanna would be going by
tomorrow wasn't difficult to predict. But I went to
sleep anyway.

* * * * *

My mother keeps the house above Cedar Lake for
solitude, for work and for me. And for my father
who is now only an occasional visitor in it. His
affairs are his own, as my mother's are for her. And
yet this small house remains a special, necessary
sanctuary for him as well. There is a bond between
the three of us that was, I suppose, created by the
abrupt disruption of our lives; a kind of amputation
from any meaning we had known before, leaving us
with experience still to be understood. Something
that lies there in each of us that only we know
about and that we really cannot yet share with
anyone else. The lives we live now are being crafted
around all the processes of creating new meanings
for a new time, a new place.

We sat over coffee, my mother and I, in the
sunshine and warmth of the small closed porch
overlooking the lake and the houses across it trailing
up along the streets that climbed the hills around
us. My mother is a handsome woman. With her fair
brown hair and Norman blue eyes, I expect she
confounds the conventional image of French women.
Self-possessed, intelligent, wise and nicely balanced
by a sense of humor that has kept my father and
myself as sane as we can claim to be. I'm sure she
has seldom doubted her own sanity, but of course
that comes from not having ever put much value in
judgmental postures. She is also enormously gifted
and not at all given to false modesty about it; well
aware of and completely in control of the
transcendent power she achieves on the concert
stage. I am absolutely in awe of that talent because

I know that I do not possess it, but I have never had my understanding of her burdened by any other awe because she has taught me to be all the rest of what she is.

She freshened our coffee and then folded a score for Erik Satie's *Trois Nocturnes* she had been working on earlier and set it on the corner of the table in front of us. She stirred her coffee quietly for a moment and then she smiled at me with the odd mixture of affection and credulous amusement that has always been one of the most comfortable things about the two of us.

"Well, you look happy enough."

"Blissful."

"I suppose I just didn't think it was this serious."

"Not exactly the kind of thing that's easy to go into detail about on the telephone. Besides, I don't think I knew myself how seriously I was beginning to take it."

"Perhaps it's time for that." She drank a swallow of her coffee and set the cup down with a small, light little laugh. "Do you have any idea how many times you've telephoned just to tell me you've met some absolutely wonderful girl?"

"Hundreds, I guess. But you've borne up very well, for which I thank you."

She glanced at me again with the same look of amused indulgence, but with a changed note in her voice and asked, "How does your Joanna feel about this?"

"That's what I want to talk to you about."

"You have doubts?"

"Not about what she feels. About how she's going to handle it, over time."

"She's very young, Vicki."

"True, and she's rather old in her way, too. But she's not had the easy freedom to put all the pieces together. Like I did."

Mother lit a cigarette with some elaboration, flicked an imaginary ash off her knee and then removed a bit of tobacco from her tongue with one finger, smiling with a touch of wryness.

"Give her freedom, Chérie. And know that you'll risk losing her."

"That's a risk you've been willing to take."

"With you, yes. I don't claim always to have been so willing."

"And with Jessi. You took it with her. And you're happy."

"We both are."

"So, if I don't take that risk, I may lose my own freedom it seems to me."

"Of course."

There is a kind of weight that seems to settle in my mother's eyes whenever she alludes to freedom. An abstraction with but a single definition, freedom is alien to experience that has dulled the edges and altered the form of what she alone would have more purely shaped. She bore the burden of my father's independence of choice and constant need of support with a compassion balanced with the preservation of her own choices. The freedom she has finally given herself and that she has insisted should be mine is a nurturing of strength necessary to her soul. She gave herself to Jessi for love. With that, she has salvaged all that was possible.

"I guess I'm having trouble imagining what a really dependent Joanna would be like. I wouldn't want to see it. She's being a baby right now about not wanting to be alone in that big house over there haunted by a lot of ugly unresolved things. She's bold enough inside the sybaritic shelter Aunt Beatrice provides, but each step toward me is an astringent leap, believe me. She gets a little giddy."

Mother crushed her cigarette out in a small crystal ash tray, her light lovely little laugh restored.

"Be patient. She's falling in and out of all kinds of needs now. Even *une petite besion d'aimer*, perhaps?"

"I just don't want her to fly into a million revealed pieces all at once."

"Dear Vicki, you're getting analytical."

"Joanna has reminded me that I'm feeling just a little less easy in the world myself. Like her, less comfortable with hiding."

She looked at me for a moment and then with comfortable, familiar simplicity ended my little dance with disquiet.

"Darling, Beatrice Fröeling telephoned me yesterday."

We talked about all of it then, but it didn't entirely relieve my concern. I sat on the edge of my chair and reached for the score Mother had set aside and without looking at it rolled it tight in my hands. She smiled and lit another cigarette. I don't like feeling foolish for having employed theatrical gestures. They tend to handle me; something my mother reminds me of when she finds it necessary. Forcefully, but not without a certain humor.

"Perhaps it would be better if you let me do the mothering, Chérie."

We were silent for a moment and through it we

both heard a car door shut on the street below. She
looked at me out of the assurance of what she had
been reflecting on in her own mind, and then
walked to the windows to look down into the street.
She smiled and turned back to me and said, "Your
taste has certainly matured."

"That sounds like something Aunt Beatrice would
say."

"I think it's time all three of us went to see
Jessi."

"I think you're right."

To say that my mother was entranced, just a
little dazzled maybe and certainly approving would
be to say little enough. For her part, Joanna had,
out of need or curiosity or a trusting relief, set aside
her watchfulness and placed herself in the hands of
her own intuitive gods as she had done that first
afternoon with me. My mother neither disappointed
nor challenged her. She simply let Joanna seduce
her. All, I think, in the space of time it took to
greet her within the clasp of both her hands, the
embrace of her look and one simple remark.

"Joanna, I am as fortunate as Vicki."

My mother's house is part studio, part museum
and part repository for a sentimental and not
unprideful collection of memorabilia of years of
concert appearances in Europe and England.
Photographs of friends and lovers, of herself, my
father and of me. Gifts from friends both famous
and infamous, oddments of furniture and rugs. The
rattan on the small glassed-in porch where we have
our morning coffee came off the lounge decks of the
old Mauritania. The piano was used for decades in
the now demolished Minneapolis Opera House. And

throughout it all a great gaggle of books and paintings and small china pieces most of which my mother had, with a foresight characteristic of her, shipped to friends here during the year before we finally left Paris.

It is a gently cluttered place, but a place of work, exuberance, and stimulation. Some of the most important things I have learned have been gifts to me from her, in that house, at that piano, where her exacting concerns for the aesthetic of my technique or the quality of my counterpoint is surpassed only by her concerns for my soul. My own room upstairs is tucked in under the pitched roof with a row of casement windows that open out to the small, wild garden at the back. A bath adjoins back to back with another for the other bedroom at the front of the house. My mother's bedroom and bath is downstairs overlooking a noble stand of Norway pine at the side of the house. The wall of the narrow stairway leading upstairs is a clustered gallery of small paintings and concert posters.

Joanna was lagging behind me on the stairs and had finally stopped altogether, her hand on the rail, gazing at a poster of my mother's last concert in Paris in the winter of 1938. Large and rather somber, a quality of sadness and loss about it, it is simply a magnificent drawing of her at the piano, bears only her name, Albertine LeBrecque, in a rather defiant red, and a single line of type at the bottom. The original art hangs beside it and is inscribed to her.

Joanna had leaned back against the wall, her arms folded high across her chest. She turned and looked up at me for a moment and after taking a deep breath, she came up to the top of the stairs beside me.

"What happens to you with all that?"

"There's a lot more to her than that."

"For you?"

"Yes, a great deal. Like your being here, for instance."

"She gave you to me down there."

"She intended to."

We had walked down the short hall and when we stepped into my little pitched-roof room, Joanna smiled and held her arms stretched out of her jacket sleeves as though to touch the opposite walls.

"I can't believe this." She dropped her arms to her sides and watched me for a small moment more and then she reached out and touched my shoulder with her fingertips, the familiar soft smile gentle, embracing all of me. "She's given you this lovely little dove côte knowing that?"

"My mother knows all there is to know. She's always known. About me and about herself."

"It's a good thing I met you first."

"You move very fast."

"I didn't mean that. It's just that it's a lot to know about all at once."

"No more than you know already. Just a wider horizon than Aunt Beatrice affords."

She slipped out of her jacket and sat on my bed. "This is wide enough for now. Come here a minute."

Minutes like that with Joanna were often elaborated yet shy little êntre-acts; gracefully sensuous, gently suspended promises she seemed to use as much for a concentrated assimilation of new knowledge as an expression of love. She had a positive and quite natural need to translate the workings of her mind into the delights of her body, or conversely. Ecstasy was ecstasy for Joanna; of mind or body, it was all one. She regarded most dichotomies as quite temporary states. I suppose because I recognized that, I found it less than honest to resist.

"I might have guessed you'd be tucked away in a lovely little room like this. May we stay here forever after?"

"Tomorrow we can go back to your house and pick up our things. Do you want to let anyone know over there?"

"No. But I would like to call Aunt Beatrice and tell her we're here."

"Yes, I guess you should. Did everything go all right downtown?"

"Like Aunt Beatrice said it would. The house is mine now. And Mother's house I told you about. All the rest when I'm eighteen." She propped herself up on one elbow and reached a hand across to lay it flat on my stomach, looking at nothing in particular and then finally at me.

"All the rest." She repeated it in a voice so tentative, so expecting of some answer, the nature of which seemed so unsure that I didn't know whether to let it lay as a statement or accept it as a question I could answer only with a compromise I wasn't sure I could make.

"It's not for me to say. About any of that."

"I don't think that's true any longer."

"True or not."

"Why not?"

"Because you need to think about everything a lot more."

"And so do you."

"I have."

"I know you have. Some."

"Joanna, I think you're asking me to live with you."

"What's left to ask, Vicki?"

"The most important thing of all. You're asking for my whole self."

How is it possible for anyone to reduce complexity to such simple terms? Maybe that ease of choice lay in a shallowness of perception at odds with her capacity to savor all the layers of cause and effect, when she considered the multiplicity of choices in all other things. Or perhaps this heedlessness was just another expression of what I was beginning to recognize as an absolutely innocent assumption; an unquestioned reality as natural as the flow of the blood in her veins, that wealth and caste and inherited privilege made all things possible, and to question this sublime rightness would have astonished her and caused her to wonder if I was thinking straight. It struck me then that Joanna was an almost incomprehensible fusion, comfortable enough to her, of sensitivity to my responses to her with a total blindness to my response to myself.

All of this would have been less difficult for me had I ever before truly considered, rather than evaded, my own capacity, or my need if it existed, to give that much of myself to her, or to anyone but my mother. Yet her presence, her easy trespass on

my life, the way she was becoming a theme whose
expression I was reluctant to develop, meant a
surrender of a sense of myself that I couldn't let go
of without first defining it.

Joanna was gazing at me with a quiet, almost
careful patience. With a kind of decorous assurance,
she was acknowledging a certain risk without
accepting its possibility.

"You will, won't you Vicki?"

"Yes, I know I will. Then we'll find out what else
there is to ask." And I pulled her down to me and
kissed her, very hard, very thoroughly.

"Mother wants us to go with her tomorrow to
spend the weekend with Jessi."

"Who's Jessi?"

"Jessica Ryder. Mother's lover."

"The attorney? That Jessica Ryder?" Joanna was
looking at me not in disbelief but with a kind of
amazement she usually has less vulnerably disguised.

"There's only one Jessi Ryder. They've been lovers
for the past four years. I think they will be forever.
I certainly hope so."

"Vicki, do you know that Aunt Beatrice has
known Jessica Ryder's family for the past hundred
years. And knows her?"

"And also knows my mother."

"And about her and Jessica?"

"Joanna, I don't know how it ever came about
that you decided on me, but when you did, that
decided it for me too. It would never have if I had
been someone else. When you told your Aunt
Beatrice who I was, she let all the rest happen. All
this may have been made in heaven, but your Aunt
Beatrice made sure it would answer to the practical

demands of earth. At least as she sees them. That's what she was talking about when she said she was going to shelter you."

"Of course, and she meant it."

"None of this surprises you? That the two of them have been arranging this?"

"I didn't know Aunt Beatrice knew your mother. That surprises me."

"Well, she does now, at least. My mother isn't exactly unknown. Aunt Beatrice called her. They had something I think she referred to as an interview."

"She is thorough."

"I don't know about you, but I feel like I've fallen down the rabbit hole."

"Welcome to the nineteenth century. It's kind of a nice place. I've been living in it for the past year and a half."

The next morning as we left the house, my mother lingered with us at the door. Joanna leaned over and kissed her cheek and then looked at her with the broadest, happiest grin I think she had ever allowed herself.

"Amazing," she said, and pushed me out the door. And ran down the brick steps ahead of me to the car.

There are certain stores that attack my good sense. Unlike my mother, whose grandeur disdains that seductive glitter, I am adorned by it. Eager to submit my plainness to a transforming glamor that turns me happily harlot. This feckless side of myself was something Joanna was seeing for the first time. It was an appeal reckless in its confidence. She walked beside me, embracing it, gathering it in and giving it shelter in the awareness that she is exactly

an inch taller than I. That our eyes meet by her
inclination. That we move within one another by the
gift of that inch we uniquely share. She smiled
without looking at me.

"I want to give you something."

"That's crazy."

"I know."

The carpet, dusted with mauve and blown roses,
yielded and spread again like late clover beneath our
feet as we walked to a perfume counter streaming
with light and deep with the musk that lies beneath
all fragrance. Shapes of a hundred flowers flowed out
in blown glass and each bottle mirrored the next, at
union with themselves.

"May I help you, Miss Becker?" from a coiffured
clerk, polished and intensely detailed; a voice
timbered to float just above the hum of mercantile
elegance. Joanna glanced at me, and then she smiled
and said, "I don't know what it is, but I'm very fond
of it."

"Chasse Gardé." My own preserve.

While Joanna signed the charge slip, the clerk
surveyed us with oblique absorption and then rolled
the slip into the lovely old plush and brass cash
tube, relic system preserved from an easeful past,
and we watched as it whirred up along the wires
like a dragonfly into the skylighted contrivance of
fluorescence and sunlight overhead, and then
returned to settle our business there.

"Becker is the magic word. Even here."

"Well, they do know me."

"Not like I do."

"I hope not," and she laughed and said, "Come
on."

The starter clapped impatient castanets again
and Joanna's hand was light in the center of my
back as we stepped into the elevator, her breath
warm and rhythmic against my neck as she stood
close behind me and we rose together to another
level.

I moved my hand between jackets hung in a
circle loose on their rack, looking for Joanna's size,
her color, something lean enough and straight, the
bone of the hangers inside them hard against my
hand. French flannels, soft as the down on her skin,
yielding resilience in shades of earth and grain and
finally the grey of stone washed with sulphur.

"Do you like that?"

"Yes. It matches your eyes."

"It's for you."

"You have eyes like a cat. Did I ever tell you
that?"

"Not until now."

"I saw a sweater for you," she said. "Back there."
And she left me, intent on that. For a moment I
struggled with the idea of her buying a sweater,
with what vision might be moving in her uncommon
mind, not sure her choosing would make me like it
better. I have my own image of myself. And then I
left it to trust, returning to her in my mind and
found the trousers I wanted for her, measuring the
size of her clasped in my hands, the fit of her in my
own contour.

I have concluded that people like Joanna are
simply perfect as they come, and would be better
clothed as the hills are, by nature. In sapphire,
garnet, the loam of earth and the dry dusk of sun
baked wheat; colors and tones all uncreatable in

fabric unless they come unmolested by the tinkering and design and the dyes of men.

I had never before dressed anyone but myself. And no one had dressed me. Not like that. Joanna came back bringing the richness of cashmere and raw silk in her arms.

"This is what I was looking for." She had folded two sweaters and a shirt carefully together and held them out to me. "Sometimes there were days when I would forget to shoot, and my father would get mad as hell and yell at me. In the fall when the sun was so bright you'd think you could hardly see. The dogs would run between the shocks of corn and flush the pheasant out against a sky as blue as glass and they would fly low and smart against the scrub and shake the milkweed loose to drift away on the air. These are like that. Like you are," and she put them in my hands.

Listening to Joanna was like listening to experimental music. Distant, crude, mockingly vernacular, with unaccountable flights into innocent, abrupt beauty; abandoned by rash choice, exposed and uncertain. Then bursting containment in a dizzy release whose intoxication falls away like a fragrance lost in the air.

"Shall we try all this on?" She nodded and followed me into the dressing room. I closed the door and set the lock behind me.

"Are you sure I should wear this to Jessi's?"

"Not on the way over there, no. Aunt Beatrice would think I was a bad influence."

"I'm not sure I'm going to like this weekend."

"There is a risk you'll be propositioned at least. And I dare say you'll like it."

And she stood approving and for approval in front of me. Splendid in narrow sulphur-grey stove pipe pants, double breasted jacket buttoned low across her hips. Under it the striped blue silk shirt which she would have left open to the navel if I had let her.

"You're an odd mix, really."

"I thought you liked me that way."

"I just want you for myself."

"That's being very possessive."

"Precisely."

It's difficult to concentrate, laughing and kissing someone at the same time, but we managed.

Jessi Ryder's weekends seemed always to be a congerie of mismatched people moving rapidly around one another like exotic fish introduced suddenly to a common tank. These haphazard mixtures were, as far as I knew, innocently enough assembled. The results, whether predictable or not, were both appreciated and used.

Yet there was at these events a very definite stratification. Levels of intimacy imposed by a deceptively loose selectivity assured that any given night would be open only to Jessi's closest lesbian friends and her past lovers; or could include other gay friends, however many strays and other waifs that might include from the available assortment of the gifted, the successful or the pretentious.

While Jessi was happily tolerant of all sorts of proletarian pretensions in others, her own tastes decidedly favored her own caste. The principals in

her pristinely structured law firm were two
daughters of then scionless families of Minnesota and
Wisconsin old wealth. Karin-Lee Burnquist,
suffocating painlessly in a fortune of milling and
grain interests, and Maddie Tolles whose apparently
endless stream of wealth had been floating down for
generations on the same chain-bound islands of
timber, thick as the ore-boats on Lake Superior, that
provided Jessi's own. These were the friends she
held closest.

Jessi's tastes in women may have over the years
favored a certain elegance of looks and the outward
hauteur of class at the expense of legitimate
connection, but she had nevertheless maintained a
fine line. Some reasonable level of independent
means, and independent thought fulfilled the
remaining requirements outside of bed. That she
found it necessary to discover the withered branch of
an aristocracy lost to time and penury in my
mother's Parisienne family was a matter my mother
tolerated with amusement.

Four years before, at a small, private and rather
select party given for my mother following her first
concert performance in Minneapolis, she had asked
to be introduced to Jessi. Mother had seen what she
wanted and simply laid siege to fulfill a need that
she had satisfied with reasonable happiness more
than once before and which she had never hidden
from my father, nor, least of all, from me. In the
cab that evening driving home, she laughed with
considerable amusement at a remark I had made
when she had introduced me to a slightly
incredulous Jessi Ryder. It seemed fatuous to suggest
that possessing a daughter like me was an

unbelievable achievement for my mother and I had simply said that Jessi would find that my mother had never failed to achieve exactly what she wanted and I didn't expect that she would fail in the future. I was fifteen at the time.

I wasn't sure then that I particularly liked Jessi, although I readily agreed that she was very handsome and had an incredibly shy and gentle voice for someone reputed to be an overpowering courtroom adversary. I remember now leaning back in the cab and folding my arms in an adjudicating gesture asking that I be allowed to reserve judgment. Mother had smiled at me, acknowledged my prudence and mockingly deplored her own lack of it.

That their love for one another is deep, passionate and abiding is beyond doubt in my mind now. It overflows with respect for one another, great humor and just that sense of irony that has helped them survive the few duplicities they have let be forced upon them. Their separations are short, infrequent and matters of surface, untroublesome accommodations to the pattern of their professional lives and uncompromisingly adhered to.

That afternoon Jessi greeted my mother with a warm, elaborate and somewhat self-conscious kiss which she returned with a touch of humor. Meant, I suspected, to relieve Joanna's uneasiness and reduce the chance of Jessi's greeting for me suffering the same overheated expression. I'd not seen Jessi since I had returned from Europe five months before. She settled for a hug, which I was happy to return, and was interrupted in any comment she might have made by Mother's remark as she glanced around, seeing the dining room table already set for ten.

"Darling, you swore this wouldn't be a mass meeting."

"And it's not, Albertine. All very benign, as promised."

"Very well, I've my children to consider. Jessi, this is Joanna."

"Joanna, I'm one of her children too, sometimes. You're welcome here on your own terms."

"Thank you. I've set no terms."

Probably no two people had ever appraised each other so quickly and so accurately. Jessi may have concluded earlier that she had a head start on that, being privy to information due oligarchic privilege and briefed as she surely had been by my mother. But I doubt that she was quite prepared for either Joanna's reply or her self-possession; and certainly not her appearance. Her remark to Joanna was made in her customary quiet, shy voice, her smile was as it usually was, disarming, suggesting vulnerability; but behind the look in her eyes lay that unimpassioned brain that never misled her, never erred on the side of sentiment.

She stood for a moment with her arm around my mother's waist, gazing intently at Joanna and then she said, "Vicki, the front rooms upstairs have been made up for you and Joanna."

"You're making me feel distinctly arrivée."

"God, Darling, you will forgive my worldling daughter."

"I'm more inclined to applaud her." And she

started up the stairway ahead of us, pausing only long enough to kiss my mother again and advise that she stop by the kitchen to make sure that the moûsse had been prepared to her liking. And to pick up my handbag leaving Joanna to carry her own.

Jessi's attentions were laconic, lingering, and deliberately assessing of the lovingly lavish front guest suite, with a quite needless review of all its amenities. Had the smallest convenience, the least necessity been overlooked or out of place, she would have known of it that morning and any oversight would have been rectified. And assessing of me, seeking perhaps more outward signs of some great leap forward into sober maturity, seriousness of purpose, or any other manifestation of abandoning the wasteful romanticism she had always felt to be my most unfortunate, if forgivable, trait. And of Joanna, about whom she knew much and at the same time very little. For although Joanna came from very old and familiar and carefully circumspect ground, she was new, fresh and intriguing territory. There would be a great deal of probing to do. In Jessi's good time. And with a discretion I felt quite sure she was already honing to a new and scalpel sharpness.

"Let me know if there's anything you want. That I can give you, of course." And she walked slowly across the room and half-closed the shutters on the glass doors leading to the balcony, and turned with her back against stripes of sunlight and color from tiers of potted flowers outside, her hands in the pockets of her flawlessly tailored white trousers. "It's good to have you home again, Vicki."

Jessi was fond of order, especially the making of

it. Her apparent ease, her tolerance for the
ramshackle spontaneity of the lives of others around
her about whom she really cared, the seeming
heedlessness that determined their days was all
material to challenge her sense of mission to set
their lives aright. And while she was generous often
beyond bounds, and flawless in her judgments, it
was difficult sometimes to avoid the helpless feeling
of being not quite fast enough on your feet, not
quite nimble enough of mind to have kept the
initiative to yourself. I lacked my mother's gift, and
her necessity, for staying just that one step ahead of
Jessi.

Joanna had been quietly surveying the room and
just as quietly assuming again her mantle of
watchful reserve, an air of thin, cool caution not lost
to Jessi and which I knew she was determined to
break through. It had never before occurred to me
that Jessi's own image of herself had within it a
carefully nurtured model she meant to bestow when
the right moment, the right opportunity and the
right well-bred girl of the prescribed cast of mind
came along. It was obvious that opportunity had
come. And I couldn't be sure that some sense of that
had not begun to uneasily enter Joanna's mind.

It seemed best to comment on the subject at
hand. "Thanks, it is good to be back. Europe was a
little sad. And depressing, I confess."

"And Duluth was cold."

"Not exactly."

A soft glow of embarrassment rose in Jessi's face.
By design or honest reaction, I cannot say, but she
recovered enough to assume her shy smile and with
it the charm that it was uncharitable not to accede

to. "No, I guess not." And she gazed with a certain patient confidence at Joanna who had about reached her level of tolerance for what she would assume were remarks deliberately meant to invade her inmost being.

"No," Joanna said, "my Great Aunt Beatrice's terms are very generous, too." And she shook her head and laughed in a light and surprising way. "Imperious, I think is the word, but generous."

"I know," Jessi said simply. "She's made things very easy for all of us." She paused just long enough to let her laconic smile soften the brittle edges of Joanna's wariness and added, "We'll see you downstairs at five-thirty," and left us.

"She's scary."

"Jessi? Come on, Joanna."

"Couldn't we just stay up here and hide under the covers?"

"Not much chance of that. Besides, how can I show you off if we do that?"

"I'd rather make love."

"You're nuts."

"Absolutely. My way of showing off."

"Maybe we should try the shower."

"I might as well say I admire your practical mind, too."

"Duty and pleasure. There will be a strict ordering of activities now that we're in Jessi Ryder's house."

"She said we were here on our own terms."

"Cocktails and brilliant conversation at five-thirty, dinner and dissertation at seven-thirty sharp. Guests will include Karin-Lee, Maddie; Valarie Chase and

Angie Richardson, Bobbie and Helene Gordon. You and me."

"They both have the same name?"

"They like it that way. And drop-in guests later in the evening. No one to worry about."

"I thought your mother objected to mob scenes."

"There are mobs; and mobs. I have exactly two-twenty-five. That gives us three hours and five minutes."

"What are they going to be doing? Your mother and Jessi."

"Issuing orders and making love probably."

"I'm beginning to like her better."

Joanna reached out and turned on the clear amber lights over the tub and shower and was naked and splendid in front of me before I could finish undressing.

We stood together under the shower and soaped each other down with gentle solemnity, a quiet expression of love and unhurried anticipation heightened by the continued surprise we shared at our own nakedness. The water streamed over us washing us clean as rain would have done and we glowed like new copper in the amber light.

That Joanna's arms should be around me, that her kiss should be deep and sure of my response was as natural as the shape of her body matched to my own; as the knowledge in her hands, her gentle grace as she sank to her knees in front of me. Until she clasped me with both arms, her face pressed against my belly and we both were still and I reached up and turned off the water and drew the big white towel from the shower glass and put it over her shoulders.

Dry and fresh and newly warm on the great wide bed in Jessi Ryder's best guest room we made love. Exquisitely absorbed in each other. Saturated with each other. Sublimely happy and confident and complete in our delight, we lay together on clean coarse linen sheets, the kind I had known once in Italy; the bars of a rainbow sunset lay over us from the half-closed shutters across the room.

Joanna lay full length beside me, leaning on one elbow; watching me, roaming over my body in easy curiosity. An apparent consideration of the shape and uniqueness of nakedness and her own privilege with it. Cherishing it in the mirror of her smile.

"You stretch like a cat, too. In lovely ripples."

"There are a lot of cats like me in Paris."

"I thought they all got eaten."

"Wrong war. Sometimes I think you've come out of some marvelous time machine. Wisely innocent, unassailably vulnerable. You're all tangled up, *ma petite bichette.*"

"Private words again."

"Untainted."

So I kissed her and left a promise with it, and reminded us both that it was already very late in the afternoon.

With Joanna at my side, I started down the staircase where precisely at its curve sweeping us into full and unfailingly commanding view, she paused, one foot resting on the step behind her, and lit a cigarette with unabashed theatricality. The probability that we were about to be devoured alive seemed not to have crossed her mind. If she had not then looked at me with a smile that barely controlled a burst of laughter, I think I might have killed her on the spot.

She examined the cigarette as if it were the first one she had ever smoked and were trying to think of a place to hide it. "Now what do I do with this?" she wanted to know. "You figure it out, nitwit. Oh, Jesus, but I do love you just the same." "That's Mother, remember?" "Oh, Mother." And we managed to get to the bottom of the stairs where she recovered something of her usually sane dignity and walked straight to the couch where my mother sat, and with a dazzling display of self-possession kissed her on the cheek, just close enough to the lobe of her ear to raise the comments I was well attuned to hear.

"Lord, what Valhalla did Vicki plunder to carry off that?"

"Duluth, I'm told."

"Something has certainly eluded me."

"That, Valarie, is something you can't expect us to believe."

"Patience, Maddie. She's repenting, for the time truly is at hand." That remark was Karin-Lee's, the cool calculations of her mind fortified with practical observation having long ago set the allowable limits of Valarie's predations. Karin-Lee's overseer stance had firmed considerably through the years as she assumed the moderator's role between distracting emotional interludes and the preservation of professional decorum at Ryder, Burnquist and Tolles: Attorneys at Law. She viewed the one clouded facet

of Jessi's nature as an unfortunate flaw, Valarie as
its most stormy manifestation; my mother a fitting
and, she hoped, a permanent setting.

Valarie is one of the natural illusionists of this
world. She seems larger than she is. She endows
flamboyance with the simple-minded faith of a
monarch mingling with the peasants. She elevates
misinformation to the level of incontestable credibility
and acts with sublime confidence on it. And reflects
upon the results with the happy conviction that
learning is everyone's gain. Believers in good, credit
her with harmlessness. Others are more watchful.

Mother was holding Joanna's hand, keeping her
close, looking as though she were quite prepared to
clasp her around the knees to keep her at her side
should such restraint prove necessary. For Valarie
had already imagined the diamond in Joanna's navel
and took the shortest way across the room.

Angie finished a long, attentive swallow of her
drink and followed Valarie to ground her for the
unnumbered thousandth time in their lives, pausing
long enough to put an arm across my shoulders.

"I'm afraid the beauty of the younger generation
is about to give Val a serious attack of anxiety.
Relax, Vicki."

"I'm having no difficulty."

"God, I don't know how you could be." And she
continued on to monitor Valarie with practiced
courage.

I do not like difficulty; just discovery. I like
having the confidence that allows me to stand in a
familiar place and enjoy a happy if transient freedom
from harm. In the shelter of the world my mother
and Jessi have made, in Jessi's house, at Jessi's

parties, I have that. I can be a spectator of my own satisfied involvement in a place of my own choosing.

For a while there is a kind of random movement that goes on at parties like that. A ritual necessity among women whose processes of selectivity among friends are complicated by considerations that both diffuse and enlarge upon their sexual pursuits.

So, the cast of meaning in a glance, the gestures that define the promise in a pair of beautiful hands, the curve of a spine as it takes the weight on an admired hip; appraising eyes, promising mouths and brows that grow to accent fine bone. Speculation invites expectation, unmarred by the dullness of impossibility. All things are a feast. And no one there is uninvited.

I simply stood, enjoying it all, sharing Joanna with intemperate pride. Valarie savored her a morsel at a time, leaving Joanna, released from my mother's grasp, waylaid by enchantment; each perceiving the other in ways distinctly remote from congruence.

Conversations hung on cigarette smoke, drifting and fragmented and I caught them and let them go like all pleasant sound we think it safe to detach from, until we sense the loss in some later disquiet. Jessi moved in dutiful calculation with each shift of these trails of smoke and mummering talk, sometimes following them, often commanding their changes into splashes of soft light and color and fragrance like some marvelous Monet I could see forming and reforming itself within the room.

Helene and Bobbie Gordon, always together like gnats in the air, smelling faintly of horses and the recent splash of Tweed cologne.

"We loved Paris." Bobbie earnestly wanted to

make that clear. "God, remember honey? I think we bought violets for each other every day we were there. Used to sit with them on the tables at Deux Magots and drink Vermouth Cassis until they wilted in the sun."

"Then we'd just go right back and buy some more." Helene clung to Bobbie's arm and then she walked right out of her mind to go buy violets. "All day it was like that," she said. "It was different at night, though."

It probably was true. I mislaid Joanna for a moment, found her again with Karin-Lee and Maddie and lingered for a while on the straight line of her shoulders, saw Jessi leaning over the back of the couch sharing my mother's laughter and then taking the empty glass from her hand. The violets wilted on the table at Deux Magots and in the little crypts of remembered shock along the walls all over Paris today. Price of resistance. Bobbie looked thoughtful and hooked a thumb into her belt, fingering the gold buckle with her initials on it.

"Well, I guess when you're born there it must seem changed a lot now."

"I don't think wars change Paris. If they change anything."

"The whole war thing still makes me shudder," Helene said. She swallowed the rest of her martini and shuddered all over again rather peevishly, I thought. "I'd just like to forget it."

I thought it best to let Bobbie reflect on that choice and cast about for Joanna again. Helene found her before I did, gazing with steady penetration.

"I never would have dreamed that skinny little dyke would turn out to be so damned gorgeous."

Bobbie seized that remark with restored authority to account for Helene's sudden leap into coincidence.

"The Beckers keep their horses at the same stable we do, you know." No, I didn't know that. "Helene has an eye for them at any age, don't you, honey."

"Look who's talking would you. You're the one who used to poke me all the time and say you just knew she was gay. Couldn't wait for her to grow up."

Bobbie sloshed her drink around, watching the ice cubes chase each other.

"Just as well to wait," she said. "With that father."

"Oh, he wasn't so bad."

"Well, he sure used to ride her plenty hard about how she handled the horses. Her hands, her seat. He used to put a silver dollar on the saddle and work her in the ring for hours until she learned not to lose it."

"You can't do that yet," Helene said. "Anyway, she got his looks. And a lot more than that by now I guess."

"Without any help from you," Bobbie said. And then she looked at me with a half-apologetic smile. Perhaps she thought it was necessary to reassure me on that point, but it was also clear why Joanna hadn't mentioned any of this. She just doesn't talk about things she has yet to sort out in her mind. Discretion in some things comes very naturally to Joanna. She just didn't need that kind of support then. She must have recognized it, but she knew she could save its embrace for another time. Apparently, Joanna had a far nicer sense of the balance of things at that point than either Helene or Bobbie had perceived. That happens when there is nothing to justify.

But whatever the nature of their acquaintance with Joanna had been in the past, it was now obviously my obligation to enlarge upon this new and finally appropriate one. The casual considerations were over now. It was time for me to gather up what was mine.

I caught Joanna's eye again and with it her amused and empathetic little smile. She set her empty glass on a coffee table and came to stand beside me as though she knew she was about to be offered up.

She nodded to Helene and Bobbie and then she put her arm around me and nuzzled my ear with a shameful confidence and one whispered remark. "It's okay. They have good taste in horses."

And she took Bobbie's hand and gave Helene a look that must have undressed her with delight. "I'd like to try your mare some morning," she said to Bobbie with an expression of incredible schoolgirl innocence. Helene's breathless giggle left Bobbie to cope with an annoyed frown when she had meant to smile and a speechlessness that Joanna gallantly overlooked by suggesting that the four of us ride that very Sunday morning.

Once again I found myself seeking metaphors in the movement of passions as Jessi's dinner party drifted into coalescence. The pattern gravely altered, everyone seemingly drawn by some long established nexus as dancers are drawn on a ballroom deck at sea following the direction of the heave of the waves. Or like gulls, circling their appetites. Jessi became the center around which everyone moved, disposed in an appearance of the most casual gravitation, yet predestined as the formation of crystal; each nurturing a fantasy newly faceted for that evening. Or the satisfaction of shattering one.

She stood as usual at the head of her table, my mother opposite her. Karin-Lee and Maddie held their flanking positions on Jessi's right and left. Their assessments of Jessi's vulnerability were mutual but contrary. Bobbie and Helene, tied together like two butterflies on invisible threads in the air, settled fitfully beside my mother, across from me where I sat as I always did.

Whatever other schema may have lain in Jessi's brain that night alongside this regular pattern of seating, a certain covetous strategy in it was not accidental. Angie had mixed the necessary signals from Jessi with a fresh martini for herself and then walked with angled certainty to the chair next to me, Valarie firmly beside her. This left Joanna rather neatly appropriated in a maneuver she responded to with a considerable, if wary, charm. She might balance Jessi's caretaking with Helen's heavy delight at finding herself beside her but I wasn't sure I could. She seemed a very long, uneasy way down the diagonal of the table.

Whenever Joanna had ventured beyond the sheltering climate of Aunt Beatrice's intellectual vigor and mandatory propriety, she acknowledged with self-possessed tact all claims for as much space as she reserved for herself. Yet that, it seemed to me, was fragile preparation for exposure to the brittle sexual innuendo, the easy contemptuous assumptions sometimes indulged in at Jessi's dinner parties. To expect to hear some expression recognizing this ingratitude for privilege, let alone penitence for it, was a matter of indifference to me, but Joanna was sure to challenge assumptions and pretentions alike. For that, I was both apprehensive and grateful.

"Jessi, this is an absolute triumph. As usual, love." Valarie paused with her fork in the air and then waved it in a small aimless circle. "But whatever made you stoop to lamb?" An added remark loaded with implication of special intimacy with Jessi's preferences. With typical acidity, Valarie had set the allusive tone. My mother simply smiled in comfortable amusement.

Angie finished off her martini and put the olive on Valarie's plate. "Probably," she said, "because some doe failed to stumble over the cliffs up on the North Shore this spring."

"That's ungenerous. Jessi never arranges things like that. She only knows people who do."

Who, or what, Jessi was testing by letting Valarie make a fool of herself, I wasn't sure. I just wanted her to shut up. Angie wasn't deterred by Jessi's silence, nor Joanna's surprised glance. "Valarie, only you could point out that distinction. Nevertheless, I prefer venison. Ungenerously."

"You've always had such interesting backwoods taste, my dear."

Helene stalked the double entendre at the

expense of any intention. "I guess you ought to know, Valarie," she said, and washed the remark down with the rest of her wine.

Valarie gave her a lingering look of despair and with a nice even emphasis said, "I'll just leave that to you." Across the table Maddie poked her fork into her salad and picked up a slice of cucumber, looking at it with pained scrutiny. "I hope that wasn't supposed to be a pun, Valarie. Anyway, we all know people who do that."

Valarie wasn't going to give Helene another opportunity. "Do what, for heaven's sake?"

"What they choose to do."

"Like eating venison anytime I like, I suppose," Angie said.

"That's a good example."

"Of what?"

"Of making personal decisions about impersonal laws."

"Meat, morality and civil disobedience. Maddie, you've had too much to drink."

"I'm only suggesting that you're breaking the law."

"Right. It's time to change the damn law."

"Fine. Now we can have a discussion of just and unjust laws."

"I thought all that was settled a hundred years ago. You're ruining my dinner, Maddie. Let everybody else eat venison too," Angie said with magnanimous finality.

"Whether we like it or not. Comes Angie's revolution and goddammit we'll all eat venison."

"That's not what I said, Maddie. That's not what I said at all. There's a difference between let and make."

"Angie, I suspect your conscience is overtaking your appetite."

"Your suspicions underrate my appetite."

"Or overrate your conscience," Maddie said.

Angie watched her for a moment with the quizzical patience of a dog who's chased a stick just once too often. "Go to hell," she said.

Jessi refilled Maddie's wine glass and leaned back in her chair in satisfaction.

These skirmishes of Maddie's were always diversionary, not clash, it seemed to me. They were opening gambits shifting law and morality about to amuse Jessi and get Karin-Lee's goat. With evident weariness at having to state the obvious, Karin-Lee said, "Neither the justness of law, nor its lack is arguable here. Nor its enforcement." And then she chose her turn to run head on into this skip rope. Oblique dashes timed to the swing of the loop were not part of Karin-Lee's style. "Precedent is what is at issue. And that is also inarguable in law."

"Precedent can be shot full of holes." Maddie was putting things exactly where she wanted them. Joanna had stopped eating, her gaze concentrated on a spot somewhere in the center of the table.

"I think you are moving into sophistry there," Angie said with a great and elevated dignity. And certainly with a look of some astonishment. She had apparently said it with reckless faith in her own perceptions and the simple odds of being correct. And to reinstate herself.

"That's right, because precedent can be used by

any sophist. Ergo, precedent is shit full of holes. Shot full of holes."

"I think your argument is, too." Helene put a small piece of her lamb on Joanna's plate and then leaned across with elaborate indifference and a remarkably skillful but sadly overlooked use of the décolleté and took Joanna's glass of wine and finished it off. "There must be something else to talk about."

There undoubtedly was, if her intention was to waste words on it. And while I couldn't be sure all this was lost to Joanna, she did seem to be relying on both her practiced opacity and what I at least could see was an alertness to a likely opening into what Maddie had started. And not unaware that this, too, was expected. She concentrated for a moment more on the center of the table and then she glanced at Jessi. And while Helene was left to fondle the empty wine glass, Joanna took the measure of all the other deliberate fallacies laid before her.

"I think all legal argument is sophistry." And she balanced for a moment on the edge of Karin-Lee's sharp glance. "Maybe that's what it's intended to be."

Karin-Lee arranged her fork and then her knife along the edge of her plate, exactly parallel. "Law, all law is based on precedent. There can be no other basis."

In the face of dismissal, Joanna went straight into the familiar ground of her own resources. "That is the snake swallowing its own tail."

In the silence, she traced a row of lines with her fork on the table cloth, ending them with a gentle stab. "Who establishes precedent?" she asked, looking at Karin-Lee. "Whose precedent is valid? Yours or the one you acquire? Mine? Anybody's here? Not yet, I don't think."

"Joanna's got a point," Maddie said quickly. "But you're going to make a lousy lawyer, baby."

"Oh, I don't know. Maybe the law could use a little more anger," Jessi said. "Assuming condition precedent." And she smiled at Karin-Lee.

"Anger is hardly the work of law." Karin-Lee was less than mollified.

"No," Joanna said. "Justice is. And I don't find a lot of that in precedent."

"Now you're discussing opinion."

"Karin-Lee, I think Joanna is talking about politics."

"Politics is certainly not the work of law."

"God forbid, of course," Maddie muttered.

"Maybe I was talking about opinion," Joanna said. "But I guess when there is enough agreement on that, it becomes what you call politics. But I call it power. Just how much power do I really have to make laws? And do I really have some moral obligation to obey laws that to me are not moral?"

"Spoken like a true Jeffersonian," Maddie laughed.

"There ought to be a better definition of that," Joanna said.

"Well, kiddo, maybe you'll find one someday."

"I intend to."

"In the meantime," Karin-Lee said, "we'll have to suffer the indignity of majority thought. And power."

"Majority of men," Joanna said.

"And 'there is little virtue in the action of masses of men.'" Jessi leaned her elbows on the table, gazing at Joanna.

"Little that benefits the masses of women. And none at all that benefits any of us," Joanna said.

"Because we are lesbians. Okay?" Maddie put her arm around Joanna's neck and gave her a sharp hug. "It's your revolution." And she smiled softly into Karin-Lee's bare and very glacial stare. "But don't be imprudent, of course."

Joanna picked up her empty wine glass, set it down again, and said nothing.

Jessi had been watching her carefully, her expression a reflection of indulgent curiosity and expectation. But as she caught Joanna's eye, there was something else in it; a protective signal, an invitation to move out of harm's way. And Joanna's perceptions, being more acute than her vanity, allowed her to quietly yield her argument to the moment and let it find its own fix among all the other gathering passions constellating around her. She smiled at Jessi, and turned a glance toward me calculated perhaps to invite an assault on her vulnerability if anyone dared.

That was satisfaction enough for Jessi. She moved us to the living room, pausing only long enough at the serving pantry door to assure that brandy and coffee would appear after the proper interval.

Joanna stood close against me while I poured us each a demitasse of coffee. She hadn't spoken since she left the dinner table.

"You risked being unhorsed in there," I ventured.

"No, I just broke a stirrup strap."

"I think poor Karin-Lee's teeth were jarred with
that lesbian stuff."

"Too bad. She knows there are laws on the books
making what all of us do a felony, for Christ's sake.
Not in this state thanks to a Victorian oversight,
which is demeaning enough. But everywhere else in
this country, just about. What's she doing about it?"

"Maybe she would have been happier if you'd put
that question into lawyer talk."

"Well, I haven't learned lawyer talk yet."

"I think you have. But you can keep right on
looking pleadingly at me whenever you get in tight
spots like that. But it looks like it's my turn now.
May I glance pleadingly at you?"

And Jessi had her arm around me before I could
finish my appeal to Joanna.

"Vicki, your dear Mamma assures me you will
play for us tonight."

Joanna simply looked at me with her most
amused smile and in a gesture of true clarity
handed me a brandy, said, don't forget to come back
to me, and walked to the couch with Jessi. For a
moment I thought of turning to my mother as I had
always done whenever Jessi involved me in one of
these impromptu after dinner recitals. But I found
that she had lit a cigarette and was lounging in a
serene, and it seemed to me, deliberate, oblivion to
my situation, apparently delighting in Bobbie and
Helene who sat in singular entwinement at her feet.
Cues, I believe, are to be taken. So I drank all of
the brandy at once and while it bored its warm,
gratifying way down through the center of my
undigested lamb Provencal, I found myself thinking

about what I had been working on all year.
Poulenc's score for *Les Biches*. Why it came to mind
was clear enough.

Les Biches was the first ballet of my childhood,
before the only war I remember. Its music is a
delightful evocation of the amoral beings it cherishes.
Their magical existence still speaks to the formation
of myself and I embraced them then with the
innocent assumptions of my childhood. The beauty,
the sensuality of its dancers, the whole elegant,
hedonistic marvel of it has enthralled me since that
evening when my mother took me to see Natalia
Markova's blue velvet boy for the first time. With
each gesture caressing the ambiguity, the
inadmissible meaning of the music, she danced the
Adagietto with feral elegance across the plane of my
mind's recall.

I returned to the tall grandeur of the theatre, to
the great elaborate light suspended in crystal above
me, to the beautiful women, none so beautiful as my
mother; a goddess in command of the most glorious
music, who made it all happen and was sharing it
with everyone there. My small jealousy at that,
tempered by pride and pleasure knowing it was my
mother they must be grateful to, and now to me for
I too was my mother: her flesh, her blood, her bone.
Never had I felt so close to her, so completely,
indissolubly a part of her; some logical, exuberant
reiteration of her larger than myself alone could ever
have been.

In the deep velvet embrace of my seat, I sat in
awe and excitation, my fingers laced tight together
in white gloves, breathing a newly entrancing oxygen
redolent with the faint fragrance of the dust of other

audiences before me, the heavy, immediate scent of
perfumes and furs and long, tissue leather gloves;
contiguous, encroaching and holding the lingering
trail of cigarette smoke. A heaven of expectation of
what I couldn't yet imagine. An entre-act to bliss.
And as the curtain rose, I surrendered to the glow
of a magic dollhouse stage conjuring up from
sourceless light a stream of dance across the dark.

At the piano on the far side of Jessi Ryder's
living room, the keyboard lit only by a soft rose light
from above my left shoulder, all else arranged itself
in a distant baffle. Out of it I separated to my
purpose and my liking each unwary mind, each
receptive, unsuspecting soul and into them I poured
all the glistening power of that music. Girl who is
boy, return to androgyny. Diffuse and equivocal, the
sole expression of what I longed to restore, the
creation of what had never been given time nor
place nor being enough to exist for me.

Playing that music that night, for the first time
at Jessi's, I was saying quite completely what I
wanted to believe I had found in Joanna. And I was
telling my mother that some new part of my life had
shaped itself in a form that was freeing me from her
a little bit more.

My mother had forgotten the admirers at her feet
and was watching me, hearing in what I hoped was
a satisfied disbelief, that quite Proustian *chanson
dansée* which was for me pure glee. Performing in
my mind's eye for hers, two ballerinas whose
attraction for one another is a sensual oblivious joy;
a fulfilled expression of the music on a palpably
explicit plane.

It was then that my mother got up from her

chair and came across the room to me. And as she stood beside the piano watching me with a smile confounded by love and gain and loss, a pleased and justified conviction, I raised my head and smiled at her and then sat back, my two hands locked between my knees.

"I'm afraid it rather lacked detachment, didn't it."

Joanna and I transferred with no great difficulty to the Minneapolis campus of the University of Minnesota in the fall of that year, 1949, and we moved into the house on Lake of Isles Maria Becker had left to her remarkable daughter.

Aunt Beatrice, with a singular balance of grace and affirmation, offered to send the furnishings from the room with the oriel window. We declined, Joanna explaining with a candor I am sure vindicated all of Aunt Beatrice's admonitions against the hazards of cant, that the room with the oriel window and all that had occurred within it was a gift from her that we chose not to violate. She sent us the Khurdistan rug from the upstairs music room and provided me with a choice of whatever piano I felt would replace her own.

Two weeks, it may have been three after that, I returned from school one afternoon and found Joanna in the den off the library. She was cleaning the long, slim black shotgun and another heavier one she had brought from the house above the river. That, along with a rifle of some sort, cleaning paraphernalia, shells and whatnot which she had cached in a modest gun cabinet in a corner of the den, were the only things she had taken from the gun room in the other house.

It wasn't that she seemed surprised to see me back earlier than I had planned to be, just slightly on edge, with a small suggestion of feeling around for how or even why to explain what she was doing after I asked her.

"Jessi and I went trapshooting this morning."

"Oh? I didn't know she went in for that."

"She's done some. She'd be pretty good if she'd concentrate on it."

"But I guess that isn't what she wants to concentrate on."

"Meaning what?"

"Do you want her to take you over?"

"Come on, Vicki. Nobody takes me over."

In its way, that seemed a true statement. Joanna's watchfulness was still a formidable, if intuitive defense.

"Okay. So that was a bit nasty."

"No, just wrong, I think."

"Well, I'm not trying to make her out to be some new Svengali, but I think it's pretty obvious she'd like you to be the Crusader Ryder of tomorrow."

"Correction. Crusader Becker."

"What if she doesn't see it that way?"

"Then I guess that's my first crusade." And Joanna placed the two clean guns carefully in the cabinet, locked it and put the key under the corner of the rug.

"Vicki, I think a lot of what Jessi does may not be what she set out to do."

"That's what happens to most people."

"Nuts. It didn't happen to your mother. It hasn't

happened to you. And I don't plan on it happening to me. Whatever Jessi may have in mind."

"Did she tell you?"

"She offered a lot of advice about school. About some changes to make."

"Why?"

"Because practicing law is not the only way to change the world. Get a degree, pass the bar, but don't practice it. There are other ways."

"Like politics?"

"What makes you think that?"

"Because I think Jessi wanted to do something like that. And knows she didn't have the nerve."

Joanna has her own ways of acknowledging a point. A kind of grace lightens the wryness of her smile, and love, at least with me, tempers her infrequent experiments with rectitude. "Well, I do," she said.

"That's what she's banking on."

Joanna looked at me for a moment and then she leaned her arms across my shoulders and with a small sigh said, "I think we have a couple of mothers who want us to choose what's right. Maybe three of them now counting Jessi. The problem is, right for them or right for us. I love you. Could we eat supper before we re-shape society?"

By moving into the house with Joanna, I had moved away from my mother for the first time in my life. And however confident she may have been that the larger decisions of life were within my grasp, she pointedly flattered me and Joanna as well with mindful concern over the telling immediacies, the small but significant relevancies that either betray or gracefully reflect the direction of one's social destiny. And so, with a nice mix of delicacy and cautionary advice gained from Jessi, she made it clear just which gay bars in the city were considered within limits for us.

Limits, then, meant class distinction. A discreet admonitory venturing into public consumption and public display of all the pleasures and follies with which the world regards the admissable nonconformities. Yet a move freighted with the masks of living unconventionally, conventionally. For at the time I met Joanna, drinking and parties, if one would assume adulthood, and meeting the women you may or may not have eventually gone to bed with were almost exclusively private affairs, privately conducted. There were after-five cocktails in selected lounges sheltered by the camouflage of mixed company. Or at one's golf or riding club where the exclusivity of membership offered at least the pretense of ambiguity. An occasional discreet dinner, perhaps; "ladies" business lunches often. But it was a life of tight, anxious decorum with as little sacrificial demeaning as possible.

At an earlier time when I followed the wayward curiosity of my mind and passions, such scrutiny of my days and nights was as remote and unlikely as everlasting love. I was loitering my way through my first year of college and while my mother remained in complete control of my musical education, I became titular head and was judged to be the most unprincipled of the small, visible group of young lesbians on campus.

The glow of benignity that hallowed such a banding together of fresh young girls during the early euphoria of World War Two was rather tarnished by then. We offered no illusion of wistful and arrested womanhood, fulfillment delayed. Times had changed. We were simply sinister, disturbing and assumed to be disturbed. But not enough to dim our delight in ourselves. With light-hearted arrogance, we made the full, heedless move from mandatory skirts and sweaters to Levis and shirts and newly discovered Mexican huaraches and went late to our favorite off-campus backroom lesbian bar. We laid shameless claim to it after the defense plant just down the river had been long boarded up and the middle-aged women machine operators who had made it their own had faded away to a sad few who gathered there to drink endless beers and make their quotas all over again with heroic nostalgia. We were a rude challenge to a better time and they left it to us finally to establish its tie to a new time and give it a new name. The Sorority House.

Whatever name it had since come to bear, it was no longer within limits. Once initiated into the self-satisfied refinements of Jessi's strata, to stray from it was to risk obloquy. Or a social cut profound and lasting. While the latter fate was, for me at least, hardly likely, hazarding the first was a temptation. I missed the rowdy nights at our Sorority House. Within that enclave social uprightness extended only to the strict absence of it. Imagination and unfettered self assurance governed admittance.

Two among us were seriously involved with things athletic, mostly golf, over which they schemed with considerable originality to achieve professional status. They were, of course, both appropriately bronzed and short-haired and given to boldness and the comforts of conversations laced with the arcane language of the golf circuit. Neither was outrageously handsome, just sufficiently attractive in a nice lean long-muscled way that represented the modest extreme of stereotyping we all enjoyed.

We also harbored one drama major who quite happily knew she was destined for character roles. A brilliant choice since she then reigned alone as a star transcending a dozen ingénues underfoot. As well as a relentless physics major gifted with a merciless sense of humor. We nurtured her with genuine compassion. A little trio of literature post-grads who looked forward with resigned gravity to life in advertising and the death of poetry. And a delightful blonde with the incredible name of Lyric Blythe who claimed to be studying to be a teacher, but who joyously made herself out as the village idiot and who looked with skepticism at all children under the age of eighteen.

There was myself and one other. A thin blade of a girl named Ántonia Branch who seemed to appear and then vanish with regularity because her father was the methodically re-elected senior Senator from Iowa. Her tenure at school was irresolute, subject to her family's constant and quixotic shifts of abode between Mason City and Washington, D.C.

Ántonia had been given that name by her mother, a dull, plain woman whose cast of glance was sharp with suspicion and whose attraction to the pretensions of a literary name saturated with the unrelenting wholesomeness of the middle-west turned out to be her only act of whimsy.

Ántonia was intelligent, dark, indolent and cynical with a tendency to sudden, sharp terrier-like attentions to any woman she found physically attractive. This happened frequently and with great intensity. I know. She was beautifully put together but fell apart, alas, with somewhat less grace; although she managed to redress this fault by a keen sense of timing tied adroitly to her own awareness of orders from home for imminent departure.

My mother was very relieved when Ántonia disappeared once more, back into the folds of her family in loamiest Iowa, thence to roam in mild boredom as officialdom demanded. But always with the lurking promise of unexpected reappearance. Mother much preferred Ann, a single-minded red-haired tennis player who joined us shortly after Ántonia's apparently final departure and with whom I enjoyed a restful and virtually platonic year.

I did rather miss those intense, concentrated wrestles with Ántonia, but they gradually became memories, elaborate with imagined joy, that I let drift off without regret. Joanna Becker had eclipsed everything.

I graduated handily, if not with brilliance, in 1950; in June, four months after my twenty-second birthday, a music major, tardy, moving without reflective pause into graduate school. That fall my mother was invited to join the faculty, a situation which provided the solace and extension of a familiar, uniquely personal shelter I suppose I still very much needed.

I had begun at last to find a strong sense of where I would fit into what I have always known my mother meant for me to be. That it has been the choice of little resistance seems a matter of martyred concern without appeal to me. I fit into it very well. I am happy and unimpeded in it; a life whose demands are rewards, whose disciplines are discovery, revelations of what has always lain within me.

Deep at work, I enjoyed an escape from the urgency of being aware and accountable to any part of the world beyond music. Enough had happened to me to last for all foreseeable time. I was well into the hermetic seal of exclusive study with my mother.

But the sands had been shifting beneath Joanna's feet. Nearly two years behind me in school but with a vision of the future clearly unlike the one I had chosen for my own and an impatience she controlled with a determination I can describe only as ferocious, she had made up her mind that she was going to pass the Minnesota Bar by her twenty-first birthday. Joanna's breathtaking sense of balance between passion and purpose had tied her then with a perceptive equivocation to Jessi Ryder. She became, for those practical purposes carefully delineated in her own mind, Jessi's creation. Yet she remained quietly and confidently grounded to the inner core of herself.

Through it all, the seemingly insurmountable work, an academic load she never would have been allowed to attempt except for the pressures Jessi brought to bear wherever it was necessary to move authority to allow it, and her Draconian tutoring, Joanna became a total student. Possessed of a single-minded clarity, a passionate, creative exhilaration and a soaring excitement that seemed to fuel itself like some delirious and exalted kind of natural force, she was remarkably happy. Her accustomed watchfulness, her practiced bleak air of resented wrongs was transcended by a marvelous explosion of confident decision.

And we loved. Nothing, apparently, would diminish the energies that drove Joanna's mind and body. A marvelous duality of intellectual gravity and physical delight. She had, more than once, and perhaps with little intended mockery, remarked that with Aunt Beatrice she had been living in the 19th century. She did seem, strangely, its child; but poised in this new time in a righteous expectation of some impending new fusion of powers, alert to their processes within herself, restless to control them. Complicated, elaborate and yet innocently unformed still. Often, with an expression of astonished honesty and a rueful sigh, she would consider the peculiar agony of confidence that comes with having the pieces and not yet being able to fit them together. Perhaps it was at such moments more than any other that I realized how much I loved her for not diminishing me.

Controlling the hours of Joanna's days, focusing the reflections of her nights, driving, demanding, cajoling, flattering, testing and assaulting by turns, Jessi found a cause and restored a few of her own lost images into the bargain. Her assessment of Joanna had been keenly calculated and I doubt if she was ever genuinely surprised by her brilliance or dismayed by her occasional collapses into numbed abandonment of her goals when the whole array of Joanna's angers would blaze fitfully and then die again, fires banked. Jessi's praise, and Jessi's empathy, Jessi's strong and unabashed embrace of this new daughter of her emotions restored the challenge for them both.

Meanwhile I kept my pact with my mother. And a vague, uneasy distance began to interstice our days and bring silence to our nights.

"Bobbie and Helene were at the stable this morning —" Joanna put her coffee cup back in the saucer and looked at me for a moment. "Who is Ántonia Branch, Vicki?"

"Is that what you've been looking for?"

"I haven't been looking for anything. But now that I've found it, I want to know."

"Helene didn't tell you?"

"With obvious delight."

"Helene always delights in past histories."

"It's present history, now."

"Only if you make it so. Why this all of a sudden? First it's my time at school. Then it's my work with Mother. And now it's Toni Branch. Ántonia Branch is someone I had an affair with a long time ago and I haven't seen her since she went to Washington or someplace. And I'll probably never see her again. And what would happen if I did?"

"You can find out. She's been staying with Valarie Chase since last week."

"I don't need to find out. Do you?"

"I don't know, Vicki. But it looks like we're going to."

Branch

I've spent a lot of my time hanging around the Neptune Fountain in the District. Our nation's capitol in Washington is referred to as the District by those who come and go as a way of attaching themselves with arcane distinction to this emanation of ultimate power. I go to the Neptune Fountain to think.

My father, Virgil Branch, is Iowa's everlasting senior Senator. He has become the ultimate fixture on Capitol Hill. There aren't many people in Iowa who have ever actually cared for the job, but even those who have, never fail to support the state's most successful beet farmer. There is a certain prudence attached to getting a thing like that settled for good.

The fact that my father's lack of scruples respecting the conditions and conduct of beet farming in this year of his Lord, 1951, has extended to the conduct of Congressional affairs, flourishing there like a carnivorous plant, as a matter of either satisfaction or indifference to his constituents. In short, he exploits the migrant farm labor imported for the purpose.

Grayed by successive layers of the dust of Mexico, East Texas, Oklahoma and Kansas, they line up their children and their women at the head of the beet rows every sunrise and end the day bent beside them black as the rich Iowa loam. They fry their evening beans and tortillas over makeshift stoves perched on the side of the ditch by the road. The battered, tenth-hand Cadillac, a heap of possessions trussed to it with wire and rope and the grace of the Virgin Mary, is nursery, pantry, what gets them to the next farm, and shade for the dogs. The ditch with a tarpaulin stretched across it is home, laundry, playground and sewer.

I no longer call my father's attention to these things because he has assured himself that people do not miss what they have never had. And besides, he insists, those who work his farm make more money than they could where they came from and they take it home to Mexico. They know the value of money. He values his beet crop in exact proportion to the subsidies successfully lobbied for it.

The Neptune Fountain was a good place to

ponder such things. Often, sitting on its edge with
my back to its neo-Greco-Roman gambol, I would
gaze across First Street and in through the front
door of the Capitol and beyond into the Senate
Chamber and imagine the gambol in progress there.
Freedom leans wearily on her sword up above, an
overlooked finial atop the dome, while down there in
the chamber she is used for ends little dreamed of
by those who stuck her up there, out of everybody's
line of sight.

The fountain is in plain sight, splashing in
glistening verdigris. Father Neptune, vacantly
morose, seemed often to gaze with me, bored
probably with those ample nymphs at either side.
Robustly abandoned, breasts erect, astride their
stallions, they remain caught in mid-plunge into
endlessly recycled water.

Considering my own next recycle, I had yet again
sought the fountain which borders the sidewalk in
front of the Library of Congress. At the time, I was
doing some ill-focused research for a book I thought
I was going to write about Argentina. There were a
few ratty little iron chairs and tables on the terrace
just outside the tunnel entrance that burrows its
way under the main steps, and zealously early one
morning for this project, I sat there fighting the
wind for my morning *Post,* sharing my paper cup of
dismal coffee with the leaves chasing themselves
around the table. I listened to the splash of the
fountain, felt the first cold drops of rain, and got
very angry about Argentina.

I went to Argentina in the winter of 1950 at the
taxpayers' expense, part of some sort of fact-finding
junket arranged by my father. My official

designation: Ántonia Branch, special assistant to
Senator Branch on the views of university students.
My own reasons for attaching myself to that charade
had little to do at the time with the publicized
investigations into threats to democracy the special
committee was up to. My awareness of its hidden
agenda, a gimlet-eyed focus on rising anti-Péronista
agitation and hypocritical cooperation with Juan
Péron's watchdogs, seemed just some more tiresome
Red-baiting — that dissent and communism were
synonymous, a simplistic notion that was becoming
an infectious disease. That February, of course, my
father's colleague from Wisconsin had turned it into
an epidemic that was to rage for five incredible
years, and that shaped me forever.

But in Argentina, then, all I cared about was
getting to the University at Córdoba, a trip of some
four hundred spectacular, emotional miles across the
grassland into the green Andean foothills. Pushing
through yellow dust mixed with the black soot of
British coal, the still, blind heat of days and stark
white moonlit nights that turned the whole
landscape around like a photographic negative, I had
both time and sleeplessness to consider the wonder
of why I was riding to Córdoba. It seemed to me
that things beginning to happen there would
someday go a long way toward changing the hearts
and minds of a lot of beet farmers in Iowa and
elsewhere. Enrolled in special classes devoted to
ferment and undigested ideas, life for me became
murky and exciting. I embraced revolution with an
easy enthusiasm. More correctly, as I reflect on it,
with an awed conviction and gritty rectitude
untroubled by dubiety.

I was pretty angry all the time I was there. The young men were brilliant enough, even charming. Confident, keen on the idea of changing places with all those old men at the top whose only exit route was death, one way or the other. Ablaze with plots to hurry them on their way. Only to quarrel a lot, rehearsing violence and falling into factions. Contemptuous, radical, and serene in a kind of professional student never-never land, their immunity from arrest guaranteed by the revolt of their grandfathers and the grace of the government police.

Immunity was their only real power. Not the threat that any arrest would coalesce the splinter groups; the fragments would gather together instantly like filings to a magnet, massing with a violent force. Their invulnerability was an article of faith.

For the young women, that invulnerability was real. They were unreachable. I remain sorry for that because one especially was lovely and bright beyond belief. I wanted to sleep with her to make my real presence known. It would have been the only valid mark I could have left on their revolution.

So there I was, sitting on the edge of the Neptune Fountain, making up my mind to go back to Minneapolis. It was an unlikely place to take all of my weary mental baggage of riot and upheaval, but there were other considerations. From somewhere out of the back of my mind had come a lot of pleasantly persistent thoughts about the gay little band of fresh-faced dykes that had terrorized my sorority house during my last brief tenure at Minnesota. As well as some particular thoughts about Victoria LeBrecque.

I had enjoyed Vicki. We certainly had enjoyed each other. Sober, serious and in thrall to her amazing mother, Vicki was open to experiment but pretty closed to commitment about any of it. She seemed always to be on the verge of finding something she was looking for, but not quiet ready, or willing maybe, to define what it was. Tales reaching me in the District suggested that she had recently found it.

Following a summer in Europe, during which I liked to think she had struggled with a lot of anguish and despair over me, Vicki had disappeared into the frozen wastes of Duluth. And reappeared triumphant from that Valhalla with its most glorious, youngest and also wealthiest Valkyrie. Anyone sensible would trust Valarie Chase with everything but her own virtue. What Valarie reports, I believe. But this new splendor surrounding Vicki was something I wanted to see for myself.

There is something appealing about Valarie's self-indulgence and supreme bad taste. She has sheltered me so often and so well and with so heedless a generosity that it would leave me quite stunned were she to ask for anything in return but that newly enlightened piece of my body she knows with satisfied conviction will be there each time I come back, battered by the world.

Finally, outside the slush and chain link fences of Wold-Chamberlin airport, Valarie met me. Big, radiant and bundled like some dazzling, jaded bear in furs of ridiculous richness. I stuffed my luggage into the trunk of her car and we were on our way to her big old house in Saint Paul's hills. She looked

over at me in a new search as we sat waiting for a
red light. "You haven't changed much. Except for
looking a little more like the devil again. Why on
earth have you let your hair grow?"

"Sorry my ravaged countenance has shaken you
so."

"Well, after all, I am fond of you. You have
despicable parents. Someone should take better care
of you. What on earth were you doing in Brazil?"

"Argentina."

"It's all the same. Full of beautiful buildings and
ugly people. A lot of Spaniards with German names."

"Germans with Spanish names. I didn't think you
knew that much about it. Anyway, I went to join
the revolution."

"Which one? There are so many."

"The student rebellion."

"I can't imagine what students have to rebel
about."

"They did seem to be losing touch with what it
was. I guess that's why I left."

"You probably left because they wouldn't let you
take over the whole thing. Here, put this out." She
handed me the cigarette holder and while I pushed
the butt out in the ashtray, reflecting that Valarie
did have a way of getting to the heart of things, she
turned the car up into her own impressive driveway
with a satisfied flourish.

In Valarie's shower, I washed away the
claustrophobia of the plane, put on clean pants and
a creased sweater and obedient to her instructions
went downstairs. She poured us each a double
scotch.

I sat down, and Valarie leaned over and kissed me. Just enough to make clear my reason for being there, not enough to start anything.

"Why do you want to see Vicki again? Is that part of your revolution?"

"Don't worry."

"My dearest Toni, I never worry. I prefer to be aware."

"This Valkyrie Vicki has carried off. When did that happen?"

"A year or so ago. No, more than that. You've been away a long time, Angelcake. And Vicki did not do the carrying off."

"Don't expect me to huff and puff and blow their house in. It's not in my plans."

"Whatever they are, you should be aware that Jessi and Albertine have them both securely under wing."

"Sounds like a good place for them."

"Oh, it is. Albertine has finally gotten Vicki launched on the longed-for musical career and Jessi is maneuvering Joanna through law school. To what end, I've no idea."

Evidence of real seriousness on Vicki's part was simply happy news, considering the talent she'd let kick around for years while she chased after girls, but Valarie's acidic reference to Jessi's interest was getting close to home.

"God, Valarie, when are you going to give up on Jessi Ryder? Sometimes I really wonder just how Angie puts up with you. Or why."

"Angie and I have an understanding."

"That's not an understanding. It's a state of shock."

"You don't seem to mind contributing to it whenever it pleases you."

"As long as it pleases you."

Valarie poured herself another drink and then she sweetened mine and just smiled at me. "When are you going to let Vicki know you're here?"

"Somehow I thought you'd already done that."

"It did rather fit into my plans."

"Okay, Valarie. Like I said, I'm not sure all of this is going to fit into mine. Besides, I haven't decided how to go about it yet."

"You can just appear. That would certainly be in character."

"Appear where? As if I didn't know you've probably got that figured out too."

"With me on Friday night up at Fran Cash's club. Jessi is staging a birthday party for Albertine. I said I would be bringing a guest."

"Jessi Ryder is giving a party in public?"

"It's like you said, love. Everyone changes if there's reason enough. It's private night, so it will be safe, I imagine."

"It doesn't sound safe to me. You told me over the phone that Vicki's nestling shoots guns. I might get killed."

"Over my dead body."

"See? That proves it. And being a clever lawyer she'd get herself off on it being a crime of passion or something."

"You're mad."

We went to bed. Valarie muttered something about how Joanna Becker probably wouldn't bother to shoot anybody because she really didn't want to be a lawyer. She wanted to overthrow the world. Now that was interesting.

Fran Cash must have been pushing her sixties by then. Or on her way through them. The place she ran up on the river across the Ramsey County line had been a roadhouse back in the twenties and thirties.

Fran was the only person I ever knew who had an autographed picture of John Dillinger behind her bar, framed by the newspaper accounts of his escape from the G-Men during a gun battle in her apartment building in Saint Paul. Fran had good connections.

It wasn't long before a select few of us who had tried our aberrant wings in the little off-campus gay bar up the river from a defense plant left over from the last great conflict, moved up to Fran Cash's establishment. Under escort. We got pinned, in a word, by Jessi Ryder's elite.

That got us off to a running start in a labyrinth of delights because Vicki LeBrecque's very own mother was holding her hand. So, we all joined hands, in a manner of speaking. The only thing that was really bizarre about the situation was its honesty. I've walked through more than one looking glass in my life. Being of sound mind, possessed of a generous nature and an enlightened sense of survival, this is one I've elected to stay on the other side of.

Being back at Fran Cash's with Valarie was a sort of déja vu of the mind, split away from the spirit. One of those blasts of recognition that displace you finally from the old image of yourself. A shift of vision. Yet, despite the notion that something in the world might have changed to match my own perceptions, Friday nights were still Cash nights there. Exclusive, invitational and devoted to the private display in a public place of the lives and loves of a dazzling array of lesbians who otherwise lived lives discreetly blended with the rest of the world.

On all other nights, bathed in genial lighting, Fran Cash was a conscious, everlasting illusion of the Hollywood cabaret girl surrounded by sophisticated extravaganza. But on Fridays, tongue in cheek and her mind squarely on a new illusion, she was resplendent in a dinner jacket of bitter chocolate brown, tailored in Italian silk with slim, narrow continental trousers to match. Hard living and a shrewd mind for business had preserved her figure for this move. But I am not sure to this day that the finesse with which she added the beige ruffle-fronted shirt, gold studded and gold linked at the cuffs, and the soft brown silk tie matched so perfectly to flat brown patent opera pumps, was just a necessary attention to detail or the exploration of a late arriving affinity. Maybe it was the small, neat, very lavender cornflower stuck in her buttonhole that made me think that.

That night, Fran roamed with a watchful eye among all of Jessi's guests, paying singular attention here and there with tact and practiced discrimination, mindful of everyone's comfort and no one's indiscretion. The young women in black tuxedos who made up the otherwise orthodox jazz quintette had wandered off the bandstand, drifting uneasily around, gold wrist watches and heavy rings deliberately apparent. In their place, a frail young man was playing a light, piquant piano accompaniment to Fran's very fashionable whiskey baritone.

She was still working variations on a number both she and that audience had always participated in. It had a free-running verse which she expanded upon depending on the mood and license the night allowed. Fran claimed to have written it, and she called it Sweet September. It was also known as "The Lesbian's Lament." Everyone loved it.

Valarie had left me and swooped off on some business of her own among the two couches in front of the fire. I watched a while as she carried on a wild conversation full of gesture and loud laughter with Maddie Tolles who was sitting on the back of a couch with her feet on the cushions between Jessi and Helene Gordon. For once Helene wasn't draped all over Bobbie. I was looking for Vicki.

She was standing by the bar, just a little on the bias, holding a drink down along one leg, clasped in her fingers across the top of the glass, talking with Karin-Lee and Angie, her gaze fixed somewhere off between them toward the fireplace. I know Vicki. She was already on her way down from Valhalla. But it would be a long time of grace before anyone else knew it. She was a little older, a little thinner, carrying just a trace of unguarded dismay. That was new.

Valarie had engulfed both couches by then, leaving me to my own devices. Vicki remained unmoved by either the commotion or having by then been deserted by Karin-Lee and Angie. She glanced again in the direction of the fireplace and then she turned and smiled at me.

"Toni, please don't just stand there looking like Tarzan."

"I could have grown horns instead of hair and caused less alarm."

"Take it as a compliment." And she touched my arm and then drew her hand away. "The South American jungle has been good for you."

"Valarie's information network tells all."

"It did get around."

"And reveals little. I was in a big city, and I was in school — when I've not been in the District. Or drifting around hearing things."

"About me."

"Do I get to meet her?"

"That can't be all you've come back for."

"No. I came to see you, I think. But it's part of the package now, isn't it?"

"Yes, it is. But not before you have a drink. And I think I would like to sweeten this up."

I got my scotch over ice and we stood for a while at the bar without saying anything. Vicki had good reason for keeping her eye on the fireplace. It required no genius to sort out who was who in the little tableau in front of the fire. Valarie draws very accurate pictures when her plans require it. Joanna was standing with her back to the fire, a drink in one hand, the other resting on the shoulder of a girl with long dark hair whose face was a picture of radiant and calculating attention. It was clear that Vicki was getting ready to advance on the situation. Things can get turned around just that quickly.

She waited until Joanna glanced up and then she leaned against my hip and smiled into her drink.

"Let's go breathe some fire."

"I thought I was going to Valhalla."

Vicki looked at me with a kind of soft, amused pain. "That's what I meant," she said.

"Don't use me for competition."

"Valarie object?"

"Vehemently. I just got back all fresh and new, remember?"

"Since when does fresh and new —"

"Don't be indecent."

"Come on."

"What if I object?"

"I was counting on that." And Vicki drew a short, quick breath. "I'm no good at this, Toni, you know that. Just be a friend. Please."

"Who's the girl?"

"I don't know," Vicki said. "Some friend of Helene's. It doesn't matter."

It didn't, really. Joanna removed her hand from the girl's shoulder with a graceful indifference, and there was nothing for calculating radiance to do but drift away with as much airiness as she could contrive.

Vicki tried hard, but she was so thoroughly in love with Joanna Becker that it seemed any move she might make would be the wrong one. Joanna simply waited against her backdrop of fire, a position I came to learn she cherished for its drama and for the way that stance had taught her to think on her feet. Some people, like cats, fight with their backs to the wall. Joanna chose fire. She just stood there, smiling at Vicki, taunting her a little, I thought, but

delighting in her. They were a lovely silence, the two
of them, in the wild clamor of that place. It took me
a long time to figure out why there was any real
trouble between them. For that moment it didn't
seem critical.

Joanna ran her hand up Vicki's back and let it
rest against her neck and kissed her softly, and then
she looked straight at me with the coolest confidence
I'd ever come up against.

"You're Toni Branch."

"Yes." It hardly seemed necessary to acknowledge
who she was.

"I hear you were down making revolutions at
Córdoba."

She had her facts straight, wherever she'd gotten
them. I glanced at Vicki fitting herself neatly along
Joanna's side.

"I'm thinking of retiring from that," I said.

"That's too bad. We could use the experience
around here."

"Toni, I think my friend here is trying to draw
you into a cellar plot."

Vicki has a nice feel for high drama and dark
intrigue, laying down false trails and assuming
disguises. Maybe this attachment to benign theatrics
neutralizes the actualities that have swept
fast-moving shadows through her own life. I guess
we all simply create the realities we can live with.

"I've been drawn into worse things," I said.
"Getting out of them was my smart move."

Joanna drew her arm from around Vicki's waist
and set her empty glass on the mantle. When she
looked at me again I realized how amazingly blue
her eyes were and that I was thinking something

idiotic like stepping out of the open door of an airplane straight into the sky.

"Why?" she asked.

"Knowing when to jump. When to change. When to change other people's minds."

"I'm not out to change anybody. I'm looking for people who don't need to be."

"Diogenes had a lot of trouble with that, too."

"Well, he had a very dim bulb in his lantern."

Vicki laughed and put her hand in the small of Joanna's back and pushed her gently ahead of her. "Jessi's about to feed us. Hush up."

"I expect we can eat and think at the same time?"

"She's unstoppable." Vicki took my hand. "Can we lure you away from Valarie?"

"Please do. She'll gather me up when it suits her."

"Does that suit you?" Joanna asked.

"If it doesn't then I'll learn something from it, I guess."

"That's a risky way to learn anything."

"From what doesn't work? What's wrong with that?"

"Know first. Then things will work."

"Not a whole lot of people doing that."

"Not many are necessary."

Vicki took Joanna's hand and walked between us. "You see what I mean?" and she gave Joanna a bump with her hip and kept herself between us. She sat us down at the table with Joanna on her right hand, me on her left. A little high, gathering her resources, Vicki was already protecting her flanks for whatever skirmish she saw ahead.

Jessi and Albertine sat at the head of the table, smiling with a reserve tempered I hoped both by the benignity of time and Valarie's unmistakable demonstration that I was the bird she had firmly in hand. The weight of their separate concerns made leaden by my past behavior on the one hand and its undecipherable direction in the present, bore heavily on the moment. Vicki's elaborate signal to her mother, that she had us both under control, Joanna and myself, was clearly meant to waylay any aroused anxiety in Albertine's mind. But it raised some uneasy questions in mine.

What possible effect my presence would have on Joanna Becker's future was a matter Jessi seemed prepared to consider at her unworried leisure. I left it to fate that she would assure Albertine that no further expression of alarm was required that night. I had all I could handle with Valarie. For that evening, I didn't want to be blown out with the rest of the candles on Albertine's birthday cake. Valarie was right. Something had happened to me. I was beginning to get fed up with my own voice. Joanna Becker, with dismaying clarity, had called a bluff I'd been using with lazy deception on only myself. Vanity has its uses, but not at such cost.

We did a lot of talking that night tucked into the corner of a couch, the three of us; Vicki finally asleep on Joanna's shoulder, she and I concentrating on the overthrow of the entire world while the fire blazed in communion with us and the mad racket of Albertine's birthday party swept around us like happy rabble rushing to face a rain of chocolate bullets in a Jeanette MacDonald movie.

There have not been very many people in Joanna

Becker's life, but I know they all, to a woman, have been completely entranced by her. Which is astonishing, really. But maybe my chemistry is unique. Never since, though, have I known anyone quite so clear-headed, determined and single-minded. They may have enjoyed the considerable passions of her body, all those others, but I was stunned by the passions of her mind. I am convinced; the excesses of a passion for one idea do ignite a revolution of the mind, and Joanna was a lit fuse running like Saint Elmo's fire toward the explosion of just one thing. Women. The world transformed for women, by women. She was just plain gone on it.

Some of this had swarmed in and out of my indignant conscience for a long time, like crazy shooting stars, flaring suddenly and then blacking out, lost in unexplored places. Or stamped out — irrelevancies in those larger revolutions hatched in the minds of men on the pampas, in sealed trains, or church basements in Boston.

But Joanna had put it all together like I'd never heard before, concentrated, condensed and volatile, ready to go somewhere, certainly not away. For some, that fire is in the genes. The rest of us catch it and blaze away in the draught. Those who don't, set backfires to watch the flame consume the flame and put out the only light that illumines the endless dark where the helix spins and wraps around itself forever.

Where Joanna had found the bits and pieces to build what spun inside of her, I did finally discover. How she was fitting them together was a process unique, unfathomable, fitful, and unfinished.

Albertine's party slowly dissolved into murmuring

knots. Vicki stirred, woke up and yawned and gazed at the fireplace and announced that the fire had gone out. Joanna smiled and pushed her carefully upright and said she was pretty sure it was still there. Vicki closed her eyes slowly and then opened them again, wide, to bring herself back.

"Toni, will you tell her to save the rest of this conspiracy until tomorrow." And she locked her arms around Joanna's neck. "Just kiss me, please, and take me home."

It looked like the world would have to await its upheaval for a little while longer. Vicki and Joanna seemed to have made the same decision for quite opposite reasons. I was the greater thing in their immediate lives. They were making me the linchpin holding the wheels on a very different kind of plot.

By the time another month was out, my bank account was ebbing rapidly. Senator Branch had hastened me out of Washington with genial largesse, but I wasn't at all confident that funds to keep me out would follow that easily. Returning to the Iowa homestead and my mother's grim pronouncements about my lack of noticeable virtues was unthinkable. And Valarie is a sanctuary I have never been insensible enough to abuse. Which meant getting back to work.

I reconsidered Argentina and the book, but let that go as impracticably remote. The whole experience was still undigested. Besides, I did not want to write a book about Argentina at all. I had wanted to write about what it meant and I hadn't

been able to figure out what it meant for me. Now,
I knew it didn't mean anything except that there
was no place for me in it; that it was not my
revolution. That made me angry, and I don't like
directionless anger. So I went, with a certain
high-minded disillusionment, where the money had
come from before. Writing radio scripts for a
side-door colleague of my father's.

This unpleasant gentleman with the aqueous
name of Breem, had fabricated an agency in Chicago
rather like molds of questionable genus are grown in
a culture dish. He had put together a formidable
and lucrative public relations firm now expert at
developing smooth, successful political campaigns in
Illinois and Iowa and a few other strategic places.
He had also continued to develop commercial radio
accounts as cover. It paid, and it was all right with
me, as well as with a few bright young men from
the Twin Cities who had gone to Chicago convinced
that Breem's was the wave of the future. I knew one
or two of them, in a riskless sort of way.

This time, I took the train to Chicago. Valarie
put me in a compartment on the Hiawatha one
night, fortified me with a small satchel stuffed with
the comforts of scotch and brandy, tins of caviar and
olives and appropriate crackers and an unmentioned
envelope where I found a hundred and fifty dollars
and a return ticket. Come back, she had said, but
get your hair cut first. Valarie's expressions of love
and concern come down on me in unsettling ways.
Incestuously, I think.

I had my berth made up early in its dinky
compartment and raised the curtain to watch the
dark Wisconsin land roll by. Stretched out on my

pleasantly swaying berth and thought instead about Jessi Ryder's remarkable party.

That celebration, I reflected, had really been a magnanimous, if selective, show of tolerance for the social mobility of the marginal among us. A coming out party for us. And for Jessi, a heady experiment with her own self-assured position. She had weighed the alternatives between the risks and the unique pleasures of public exposure pretty carefully. In its way, it was a coming out party for Jessi, too.

It seemed like she had caught the vibrations of some new restlessness in the upper air that night. Maybe, I thought, she was about to gain some sense at least that the times themselves could nail up our closet doors for good.

Fat chance of that. Jessi Ryder didn't have any problems with being gay. Just with the light. It might be a big thrill for her to abandon the path of angels, but it looked to me like she was grooming somebody else to be shot at. If Joanna Becker had been gifted with some osmotic connection to past uprisings that set her convictions about herself on the edge of revelation, then she probably would tell the whole world to go shove itself. But it didn't seem right that she should have to do it alone.

In the morning, I took a cab as far as the old Chicago Water Tower, neglected in its square of dead grass and scattered trash, and walked across to Rush Street. The air was already hot, sullen, and soggy with imminent rain. Someone in fresh seersucker and thin briefcase was standing in front of Breem's office building. Just recognizable.

"Great. Didn't know you were in Chicago, Toni."

"Hi, Larry. I hope it'll be as good to me." It was

the least controversial way I could think of to remark on his acquired corpulence.

"How's the Senator? Treating himself well?"

"As usual." He could take that any way he liked it. "I'm fine too, by the way."

"Sure, I meant that, too."

"Sure."

We stood in the elevator counting the squares in the ceiling. And then shared the unique coincidence of being summoned into Breem's office together. Larry explained that there was something new on the fire. I wasn't sure whether he was annoyed or pleased that he found himself competing with me for it. I'd already made up my mind.

Breem watched us from behind the watery opacity of his great walleyes. He was casting the bait now. Bottom feeders have nothing going for them but patience and stubbornness.

"Equal or nothing," I said. "It's the scripts you're paying for. Whether they're his or mine."

Breem smiled his big solid denture-pink smile, and lit a cigar with slow concentration. "Larry's got to take the girls out, you know."

"Well, so do I." I guess I'd also made up my mind that if anybody was going to get gaffed it wasn't going to be me.

Breem just looked at me, his big face reflected in the shallows of his glass-topped desk, and rolled the cigar on his tongue from one corner of his mouth to the other. That was his suggestion. Which I was not buying either. Larry shifted in his chair from one side of his fat bottom to the other.

"Okay. Nine. You've got it." Breem surfaced at last, but in his wake I was pretty sure I saw an extra two or three for Larry. It was the equivalent of a draw.

Maybe the whole thing cleared the air at least. Now we could argue about other things for a change. I told Breem I'd have everything to him in ninety days. According to contract.

"That's sixteen weeks delivered. And I gotta have four in here by the first, girl. The rest's in the contract."

"You're pushing hard with the four, but okay. Don't worry about the rest." I figured for sure Larry didn't have one week's worth even out of his head yet. Breem would do his worrying about that. All I needed to do was wait.

He leaned back from his desk and waved a hand. "Keep your nose clean, Toni."

Now that was just plain ignorant, but my natural generosity allows something to losers.

Leaving Chicago has never broken my heart, and that time I left it with almost exactly what I had come for. Nine thousand, even in installments, would put a rug on my newly restored floor and it was an achievement that would keep my credit good with Valarie in all its glorious variety. All I needed now was an unknown, remote and unassailable hiding place to work in. Especially one I couldn't escape from. It was time to share a little bit of the revolution with Joanna Becker.

My water glass had broken out in a beady sweat that ran down clearing the facets in the glass and making a damp circle on the tablecloth. I moved it

to a dry spot, listening to the genteel click and faint
faraway ring of silver service around us, the
undertone of murmured conversations layered with
white linen and the unconscious advertisement of a
brand of privilege as casually unaware of its own
assumptions as it was of the nature of the rest of
the world.

Vicki flattened her empty cigarette pack between
her fingers and glanced around to catch the waiter's
eye, which was rheumy and slowly responsive,
appropriate to the dining room of that particular
hotel which I know for a fact has sat there in its
intimidating affluence for seventy years while the
city gathered itself around its dim immutability.
Even the midday sun remains withdrawn, like some
indiscreet backdrop outside the long row of tall
windows cringing deep in the stone walls. Luncheon
takes on the baleful cast of assured doom, or at best,
unpromise, and a supplicant in that ambience is put
to certain disadvantage.

"I told you, Vicki. I need a place to work for a
few months and I remembered you telling me about
it. Fair enough?"

"Really, Toni? I thought you were trying to find
out if we wanted you out of the way."

"There are other sources if I wanted to know
that. Anyway, that's your business, not mine. Not
anymore."

"Yes, I'm sure there are others." Vicki gazed at
me and then smiled in that vague, secretly
preoccupied way she had. "That's sad," she said.
"One should always have one or two illusions tucked
away. For emergencies."

With a sepulchral mien, the waiter laid the fresh

pack of cigarettes at Vicki's elbow and then lit her
cigarette with a match that flared and then died
suddenly like a flame consuming the last oxygen in
some tomb.

"I guess I don't appreciate any emergencies that
illusions will get me through. Although sitting here
in this mausoleum could bring that to mind."

"Oh?"

I wasn't quite sure which of those two thoughts
Vicki was considering until she brought them
together with admirable economy.

"It does have its charms, Toni. This is the chosen
retreat of Joanna's Aunt Beatrice when she comes
down from Duluth. You'll see it that way too, since I
assume you intend to get along with her."

"That's required?"

"Definitely, if you're going to be spending any
part of the summer up on the North Shore." And
she took two keys strung on a small wooden tab
from her purse and pushed them across the
tablecloth toward me. "I think Joanna would have
liked it better if you had asked her instead of me."

"I know you better."

"Which makes it less of a favor, then?"

"It's not my intention to have it be a favor."

"Joanna won't accept money. You know that."

"You see? You're less formidable."

"Formidable." Vicki laughed. "There's nothing
formidable about Joanna." She put her elbow on the
table, resting her chin in her hand, and looked at
me with a light, rather quizzical expression. "You've
made me feel better," she said. "Your ego is showing
again. And your deprecated illusions."

"I think I've given up on illusions."

"Fantasies, then. They're the raw material of reality, don't you think?"

"I just take what's there and wrestle with it."

"Yes, I know." Vicki rubbed out her cigarette in a gentle, contemplative circle. "Shall we order?"

The waiter, who had been lurking with a vulture's eye just beyond earshot, was suddenly at her elbow.

"I think the small soufflé, and the Alfredo; the chilled asparagus; is that a lemon vinaigrette? Fine, we'll share. Will you be happy with that?" she asked without glancing at me. "And the wine list, please." Ritual tactic, elaborated and prolonged; a kind of breathing space, a time to re-shuffle the order of what was in her mind. As though she is thinking in another language, which I suppose she does, and obliged to speak in one regrettably inadequate to her thought. It is a process that reminds me to not forget exactly what I have said.

She leaned her chin in one hand again and reached across the table and snapped off a leaf from the one rose in a slim, fluted vase, turning it back and forth for a moment in her fingers. "Toni, you come and go in my life like some sort of itinerate confessor. Odd, isn't it? Does it come naturally, or do you cultivate it?"

"I think you do."

"Then I should tell you I've decided to go along on a music workshop tour this summer. Although it wasn't exactly my idea, my fantasy. It was Mother's. All very experimental. Lots of new music. Some old as well. Some neo-old. Composition, harmonic studies, all that. Mother's been putting it together all winter."

"Where?"

"Just some small schools where not much of this sort of thing happens for them. In Iowa and Wisconsin, Nebraska at Lincoln; maybe Missouri."

"That takes all summer?"

"Not really. We'll finish up back here in Saint Paul around the end of August."

"And that's just fine with you."

"It ought to be wonderful, really. A chance to perform away from here. To find out how I feel about teaching. One more of Mother's fantasies assured."

It seemed to me that Vicki was resounding with a bright apprehension, like some sort of glass harmonica that had hidden within its shimmering vibrations one empty glass that would, without warning but with unavoidable certainty, sound a dead and hollow and dismally truthful note.

"I think it's your fantasies Albertine's not so sure of."

The waiter brought the wine. Vicki considered it with care and concentration, pronounced it acceptable, and then pushed her wine glass aside, her fingers spread carefully straight at the base of the stem.

"Meaning Joanna, of course."

"I think that's what I meant."

"Yes, Mother does feel that. A little *bourgeois* unease, I think. She's afraid I'm moving out of my class with her. Either up or down is unsettling. I'm sure she feels Joanna is not apt to rove very far from her pinnacle. Nor for very long."

"Long enough for her purposes, I suppose. What does she think of it, this tour?"

"I've yet to find out, really. But I'm sure she knows I've told Mother I'll do it."

"Maybe that explains it."

"Explains what?"

"Calculating Radiance. That girl at Fran Cash's that night. How often has that happened?"

Vicki gazed at me for a long time before she answered, as though this was a thought so arcane as to be a product of my narrow imagining alone. "Joanna likes being adulated," she said.

"My guess is she likes competing with Albertine a whole lot less."

Vicki's timing is admirably adroit. Our food was served with a concentrated attentiveness; the waiter portioned everything out as she had indicated while she watched, smiling, reflective, and looking at me finally with a rather self-assured conviction.

"Joanna doesn't know it yet, but she's not competing with my mother. Not any more — if she ever was. Nor is it quite the other way around, really."

"Except that Joanna has to win."

"Shouldn't she?"

"So it's okay to leave this summer. Who are you testing, Vicki?"

"Dear Confessor — myself. That is all." And she shrugged her shoulders just a little, turning one hand palm up and then gently clenching her fingers. "*Á contre coeur*, Toni; against my heart, yes. What would I do if she was unfaithful to me. That's the quaint thing you're asking me, isn't it?"

"Has she before?"

"Before me? Of course. At least once that she's told me about."

"That's hard to believe."

"I didn't say I believed it."

"But you want to."

"No. I just believe her now."

For a few minutes we ate, each of us, it seemed, in a private, unsettled silence. I watched the small soufflé ease into an almost imperceptible collapse, each pore faintly breathing away fragrance and flavor until I cut into it and turned it then on my tongue absorbed in balancing it with the vinaigrette.

"Vicki, this place of Joanna's. How far away is it from Aunt Beatrice's?"

"Far enough, but not that far." Vicki smiled at me. "If you're fishing, upstairs was far enough. She won't intrude on you once the amenities have been attended to. Joanna and Aunt Beatrice both have a unique appreciation for distance. For necessary space. It's a state of mind with them, I think."

I turned the wooden tab over and spread the keys apart. Fröeling-Route 9 was burned into one side of the tab. Vicki watched me quietly for a moment and then she gathered up her cigarettes and matches and put them into her bag.

"It's Joanna's cabin. Neither of them are very possessive about details." Vicki leaned across the table and picked up the keys and put them in my hand. "The big key opens both doors," she said. "The other is for the garage below. It's about a half mile or so off the highway down to the lake. You'll see a row of mail boxes just before you get to the Split

Rock lighthouse. Joanna said to tell you that everything you'll need is there to hold you for the first week at least. There's a grocery up on the highway at Castle Danger, or you can go back to Two Harbors. Oh, everything except a telephone."

"The most important exception. Thank her for me, Vicki."

"No need. There'll be lots of time for that. Maybe the next time the two of you are plotting the revolution."

She got the waiter's attention again and signed the check and reminded him that it went on Miss Becker's account. He gazed at it and said thank you, Miss LeBrecque, in a hollow voice and I followed Vicki out into the sunshine. Along the flower-edged path to the parking lot, where the shrubbery grew close around a curve, she paused.

"You don't have to stop on the way up to see Aunt Beatrice. But you must, you know, Toni. In a week or so." And she laughed suddenly and kissed me. "Anything more would set the antimacassars in there quite askew, don't you think?"

I watched her walk away. I don't know why, but, still holding the keys to Joanna's cabin in my hand, I was thinking about Aunt Beatrice.

Tomorrow has got to be a greater gift than yesterday. Polishing off straightforward thoughts like that confirms my faith in those little devils that whisper *procrastino, procrastinare*. Brightened, then, and reassured, I can shave away the days for doing the praised and recommended, even the promised thing. The salvation of the soul of America's washday could hardly lie in the episodic revelations of a batch of radio scripts I had yet to write. In uprisings of the mind, however, I recognize a certain insistency. And the value of tact.

The day before I had planned to leave Saint Paul, I packed my newly acquired car and then spent the night dreaming myself half way to Duluth. When I woke up in the morning, I lay on my back and continued the journey around the wallpaper bordering the ceiling in Valarie's bedroom.

"I've got to see Joanna first."

"Whatever happened to Duluth?" Valarie was muttering in her pillow.

"It'll be there tomorrow."

"In all its tragic sameness."

"Not quite, maybe."

"Don't get too entranced."

"By Duluth?"

"By Joanna, Angelcake." Valarie says surprising things when I think she's half asleep.

I found my way from Valarie's to Marshall Avenue and drove across the river to Minneapolis and west on Lake Street, that being the only reasonable way I could recall to get to Lake Of The Isles. Vicki had given me the address, written in her vertical, very French hand, on the back of half a sheet of music paper. On the arm of the lake toward Kenwood Park, the house was backed from the street and smaller than I had rather invidiously imagined, but quite appropriately sheltered with a lot of casually tended shrubbery, blue spruce, and poplar trees.

I rang the bell, reflecting that my concerns for

protocol had weighed so heavily on thanking Joanna
for the cabin she was providing, I had overlooked
the implications of seditious purpose she might pick
up on in this unannounced arrival at her door. It
opened suddenly, wide and with intimidating
suggestion. I had forgotten about the housekeeper,
who was tall, but not large, open-faced and very
Norwegian. With a careful scrutiny that established
her obligation to either rightfully assess my
legitimacy or close the door in my face, she asked if
Miss Becker was expecting me. Not exactly, but I
hoped it didn't matter. She would verify that and
return shortly if I would please step inside.

From the big, open entryway, I could see the
fireplace and Vicki's grand piano in the living room
and not a great deal more. Ahead, beyond a stairway
that curved away into the upstairs landing, a row of
French doors opened to a veranda where the
housekeeper materialized again and announced that I
would find Miss Becker at the foot of the lawn.

The view from the veranda was down the lake to
the islands, and protectively blindered on either side
by great white-flowering lilac. Two sprawling
sycamores, mottled and made for climbing, shaded
the lawn out to its meandering border of pansies
and blue flag, the iris my mother plants in rigid
rows in Iowa. The natural contour of the slope rolled
easily down to the pebbled shore, shaping the course
of a pathway of random stones to a small wooden
dock. Miss Becker would be on the dock. She wasn't,
exactly. She was bending over inside a dark green
canoe on the water beside it, cleaning it out,
apparently. She looked up as I walked down the

path, and then she stood up and waited until I reached the dock.

She was wearing a pair of brief white swimming trunks and nothing else except a yellow checked shirt with the sleeves cut off at the shoulder and open down her chest to her navel. Looking at her then, I couldn't be sure if she was really aware of her own beauty, which was grave, thoughtful and startling all at once. I guessed not. The allowable conception of such things doesn't much celebrate the disturbing androgyny that seems to have shaped her, the ineffable wildness that threatens to let loose God knows what dangers lying restlessly in the minds of the rest of us.

She smiled at me like she was savoring a small but significant triumph, and then she pitched a cloth she was holding into the bottom of the canoe and stepped up on the dock.

"Toni, I'm sorry. Our housekeeper's circumspection is natural, I think."

"My credentials are very vague."

"They're clear enough now."

She had started up the path toward the house, taking the stones two at a time, bending over to pick up a fallen twig, and then turned to face me, walking backwards slowly, turning the twig in her fingers, flickering the sunlight off its few leaves. Joanna Becker is one of those people, intensely sexual without seeming to be exactly aware of it, who, we delightedly surmise, are very effectively undressing us when they gaze so intently all over us, but who are actually reserving their sensuality for themselves alone.

It took me some slow, careful seconds to remind myself that this was what Valarie had recognized. A kindred attraction. Valarie is fascinated with herself wherever she finds it. And she never fails to take it, untroubled by any distinction between amoral innocence and simple crassness, satisfied with a mutuality of possession she is convinced justifies itself.

I am not a natural saver of souls. I have no uncontrollable urges to set the unwise on the correct path. That is a very different thing from changing the universe. I decided right there that my own enchantment with Joanna Becker would be weaving its way around other issues.

Joanna tossed the twig aside and smiled, satisfied, as though she'd walked right into my mind, had no terrible concern for what lay on its surface and then rummaged around for what she was really looking for.

"You'll stay and have lunch with us. Right? I'd like to talk to you about blowing up the world." And then she laughed and said, "My favorite topic," and waited while I caught up with her along the path. "By the way, you'll get along very well with my Aunt Beatrice. I did a little groundwork for you."

"Character references?"

"Yes, the best necessary."

It is difficult to resist any conviction Joanna holds or has properly arranged for.

On the veranda, a luncheon table was already set. For three. A dark, low pitcher filled with white and yellow roses in the center, white napkins rolled into silver rings. Joanna leaned over the table to

smell the roses and then explained that she would
be only a few minutes. The housekeeper would never
allow her to sit at the table undressed like that. She
disappeared through the French doors. The phone
rang somewhere in the house a few times and then
I could hear her talking upstairs.

I wedged myself between a strew of pillows and
books and papers on the long, white wicker couch at
the end of the veranda. The *American Law Review,*
a pamphlet titled *Law and Post-War Society,* and
two copies of the *Minnesota Law Review*. And a
marked copy of *The Declaration of Independence* by
Carl Becker, whose name I assumed was only
coincidental. All of it mingled with the fragrance of
lilacs behind me and with Bertrand de Jouvenel and
Thucydides as they struggled with the nature of
power.

The de Jouvenel was obviously a new book. With
a few note cards slipped between the early pages, it
lay open on top of the stack: "The only obstacle that
Caesarism has to fear, is a movement of libertarian
resistance, governed by law, as a system of civil and
political liberty." This, Joanna had underlined with a
black pencil, "governed by law" got it twice. In the
margin she had written, "God! Law is men, and men
make laws that limit not the growth of their power,
but the liberties of women." M. de Jouvenel was not
faring well with her. Alongside this exasperated
comment she had added, *See S. LaF.*

She must have given up about then and jammed
the pencil into another small book tucked by itself
between the cushions, and gone down to the dock to
work off her dudgeon on the bottom of the canoe. A

reasonable act, considering that the note referred to that same small, vaguely familiar book, *Concerning Women* by Suzanne LaFollette.

Whether that name rings with sublime harmony or dissidence, in Midwestern ears it rings. It took me a few minutes to get my thoughts straight about Suzanne LaFollette and just where she fit into the District lore about the whole troublesome, tub-thumping lot of LaFollettes who lived for years in one enormous house, a sort of conspiratorial hatchery on Sixteenth Street on Capitol Hill.

Suzanne LaFollette had worked on the Hill for a while as her uncle's secretary of sorts. She had sharpened her political teeth and her suffragist consciousness in a family devoted to endless discussion and relentless dissent. She must have had enough material for a dozen books, but had distilled it with cold lucidity into one, concerning women.

I pulled it out from between the cushions and it dropped open along its cracked back where a thin gold Eversharp pencil was clipped to the page. It seemed like the whole book was black with underlining and notes written with vehement care in the margins. But there were some others, earlier and faded, in someone else's hand. Beatrice Fröeling had also written her name, and a date, 1926, on the front flyleaf. A handful of pamphlets with a rubber band around them was stuffed between the cushions with the book, a bunch of abstracts and statistics on women in the professions, working women in factories, in business, mostly World War One vintage, each pamphlet with Beatrice Fröeling's name in ink on the front cover.

Joanna Becker's path was not exactly uncharted.

Aunt Beatrice had recognized a torch-bearer when she saw one. Passing the flame along was an act of indulgent faith. Whatever it would ignite in Joanna's hands, Beatrice Fröeling must have figured to be a matter of sanguine risk. I went back to what were clearly Joanna's margin notes in the book. Argumentative, lucid, and sometimes funny; anecdotal, carefully detailed and drawing sharp and surprising relationships between ideas, including those I had to conclude were her own.

I was so absorbed in all this, I didn't hear her come back onto the veranda, still barefoot, but obviously freshly showered and a bit calculatedly resplendent, I thought, in a silk shirt and linen pants rolled a couple of times at the cuff. Maybe not. Maybe I just find that kind of carelessly casual ease unlikely without contrivance — a skepticism deeply ingrained, a result of exposure to my Iowa mother's stern fundamentalist dubiety respecting the privileges of position.

Joanna stood looking out at the lake for a moment and then she pulled a chair out from the table and sat straddling it, her arms folded on the back, gazing at me. She smiled and ran her tongue along her teeth.

"Aren't you going to ask what all that has to do with me? Everyone else does."

"Except your Aunt Beatrice."

"Yes, except Aunt Beatrice. And now you. But then, I expected you to be bright."

"Bright enough to put a few pieces together."

"And use them?"

"That depends. Right now, it's probably just protective coloration."

"You've done a lot of running into hard places just for that."

"Just looking. Like I told you that night at Fran Cash's. Making the inkwells jump is a state of mind with most people. There's a lot of comfortable belief out there in the safety of talk. Men wrapping themselves up in the cozy armor of ideas some other poor fool can get shot for."

"I don't give a damn about mens' conflicts. They're as old as time. And the same goes for the ideas behind them. They talk with the same contempt for our existence, the same exclusivity today as they've done for a million years. That stuff over there —" She gestured with one hand at the books beside me, "It's boring. Among other things."

I closed LaFollette's book on the gold Eversharp and put it on the top of the stack. Joanna just smiled. I hadn't really meant to throw it in with the rest quite like that. "Well, at least she asked the right questions. And had the right answers."

"The right answers for her time," Joanna said.

She stretched around the back of her chair to reach for a small notebook stuffed in with everything else on the couch and sat with it in one hand, her arms crossed again on the back of the chair, gazing at me with a look of amused skepticism. I don't really like being set up, even for things I might be all hot about getting into.

"Okay, so you don't believe I'm all disillusioned about revolutions. Where's Vicki, by the way?"

"All tangled up with Albertine at school. She'll be along for lunch."

"Time enough for us to reclaim the whole world

for women, no doubt. Although I'm not so sure they deserve it."

"Some do. The rest will."

"What's that? Zeal or gall?"

"Both. Plus anger and, well, maybe I like the idea of making the inkwells jump, as you put it."

"Nobody ever did that alone and got away with it."

"No, that's what Aunt Beatrice keeps reminding me. She tried it once, along with a few others. Stood on street corners and yelled. A long time ago."

"It got the vote. Give her that much."

"I give her a lot more. Aunt Beatrice was bright enough to see that the vote wasn't enough. Women would just vote the way men told them to. That's why she went back out and yelled some more. Along with a few others."

"You try that today and you'll end up in the funny farm. A whole lot of women are going to have to start yelling all over again. And they're not going to soon."

"That's why I'm not talking about yells and screams any more. I'm talking about power."

"Take over the palace, I suppose."

"Tear it down and build it right," she said.

Joanna turned the little notebook over in her fingers, bending it nearly double under her thumb, and then she held it up in front of me.

"Seven," she said. "Can you believe that? In eighteen eighty-five, Belle LaFollette was the only woman to graduate from Law School in Wisconsin. No woman graduated here that I can discover. Now there are one hundred and nine enrolled in this school of law and seven of them are women. In sixty-five years we go from one to seven. If they graduate, that is. God!" And she threw the notebook back on the couch. "Do you know what that means?"

"Seven legal secretaries, probably."

"Bingo. Right now I need a whole flock of hours in torts and briefs. For the past year those sessions have been filled with men. Men who haven't grade point to even be there, but are. Next semester I need assignment to court for student monitoring. I'm on the wait list with men ahead of me. Why? Because there are two lists. One for them, one for seven women. Guess what happens."

"You're in the middle of a mine field, kiddo."

"Am I supposed to let Jessi detonate mines for me? Sure, I can. But what about the others? They'll run out of caring, or money, most of them. They've little enough support as it is. It's time to lay our own mine field."

"Well, it took only Sam Adams and his hot-head friends to start the American Revolution." That was the wrong thing to say even before I started saying it.

"And Lenin jumped out of a box car at the Finland Station all by himself. Jesus! It's not like I'm trying to put together some kind of Communist cell. With two bankers' daughters and a surgeon's niece? Be serious. Hand me that." She pointed to the little notebook she had flung out of reach.

"Why not?"

"You sound like Vicki now. All wrapped up in the romance of rebellion. I was counting on you to remind me how ugly it is." And from the notebook she read off five names and the information on their unfortunate status, their antecedents, pausing in pained exasperation over each unlikely background. "That last one is a State Senator's child without a living brain in her head."

"That's only five. How about the heiress to the Mesabi Range?"

"Who?"

"You, Tovaritch."

She looked at me with a kind of patient indulgence mixed with what I hoped wasn't enough patrician despair to not continue. I am not at my best bending to the generosities of class, even in those who proffer them as gracefully as Joanna Becker does.

"And there's Amy Larson for six," she said. "Which probably saves it."

"From what?"

"Lack of attention. Amy is a police officer on the Saint Paul force. She's working on her law degree at night, on what leave she can get; however she can. And her mother is regional organizer for the ILGWU. Just to add a little ambiguity."

"God. A cop with true blue junior red revolutionary bona fides. Boring from within, right?"

"Somebody might call it that." And she smiled with the absorbed satisfaction of a chess player one undetected move away from checking somebody's king.

"Aren't you screwing up people's credentials with what they really think? Assuming they do, of course."

"Amy thinks. But, yes, I am trying to imagine that. It may be time to move beyond law majors."

"Like trying to get me into this?"

"I need an off-campus, non-student, ex-revolutionary advisor."

"In that capacity, maybe I should remind you there are men out there. If there are any who are not white, Protestant and upper middle-class, that is."

"Keep the men to yourself, Toni."

It didn't sound like it meant anything. Just one of those off-hand remarks. Like a stone held in the fingers. Skip it lightly over the water, or throw it; aimed.

"They've got firepower and you can use that."

"And they use it to their own ends. Not ours. I've got enough things to fight without taking on that."

"They've all got three strikes against them just because they're men, as far as you're concerned."

Joanna still sat comfortably straddling the chair, gazing at me out of a kind of clear blue certainty, and then she leaned her chin on her hands on the back of the chair. "That's right. As far as I'm concerned." Cool, no perceptible rise in her voice, just a new hone to the edge, the kind that turns to catch the hard glint of the light. "What's going on here? That's right as far as you're concerned, too. Isn't it, Branch?"

"What am I supposed to say? Okay in these circumstances?"

"Whatever you want to say. Other circumstances are your business. I really don't care who, or what, you sleep with. As long as you enjoy it. I do what I enjoy. Whether that's Vicki or fifty other women. That's my kind of funny, and I like it that way."

"So much for Doctor Freud."

"You know what you can do with that."

"I already have."

"I grew up being taught all about male privilege, and I learned how to use it. The only problem was, I am not male and I couldn't quite find any natural justification for that privilege nor any natural right to deny it to the woman I've become. To any woman."

All that time she had been holding the notebook in one hand, her thumb between the pages. She looked at it for a moment and then she closed it and reached out to set it on the edge of the couch. "I wonder if you realize what that's like," she said, and she paused to run her fingers through her hair. "To be a girl with that sort of privilege, to play at boys' games, to be serious about it, encouraged, unquestioned. And suddenly discover you don't have any right to any of it when you grow up. My father gave that to me without telling me how false a gift it was. He just killed himself before he could take it away. But others try to. Every day. It's time the assumptions behind that were challenged. Again."

"And reversed?"

"That might be nice for a change. Say for the next ten thousand years or so. But I don't think reversing the situation will solve the problem." Joanna laughed suddenly and said, "You enjoy playing devil's advocate?"

"Not really, no. But you're going to have to tangle with the men thing in all those other women in your notebook."

"Not all of them."

"Every woman is a lesbian — or ought to be. Right? You're off again."

"Yes, I am. Because one day that's where the only real strength is going to come from. Anyway, the problem with them now is learning to do something for themselves. Having a sense of their right to their own decisions. The simple, unassailable rightness of it. Like Aunt Beatrice says it has always been, girls get sold a bill of goods from the word go."

"All of a sudden it sounds like we're not talking about women law students anymore. We're talking about women."

"Bright girl."

"Jesus. We're back to a nation of women again. And power. Isn't that what you said? Do you know where most women's illusions of power lie? With men. In this world they're in a bind with men. Eating and sleeping under a roof, making babies and being approved of. It gets habit-forming, I guess."

"Autonomy is too big a price to pay for an illusion."

"Autonomy. That's a very high-class word. I don't know, maybe the way they see it, it's worth the price."

"That doesn't make it worth it to me."

"You're not their concern."

"I plan to make myself their concern."

"Then you had better be prepared to get your ass kicked. Hard."

"For blowing the cover on generations of hypocritical injustice."

"For blowing the cover on injustice. All by yourself."

"So what have you to lose? Or Jessi, or Albertine? Any gay woman?"

"You were on my back a minute ago for being the devil's advocate. Now you get to play village idiot? I don't think there's much chance at all that you or Jessi or anybody else in her little enclave would lose anything. That's a pretty carefully protected place. By money, right? Lots of it. By the prestige of a solid old law firm their daddies built. Old, powerful families that shelter their own no matter what kind of crazy, scandalous, unholy, radical things their black sheep do. That's your immunity. And mine, too, I admit. None of us are 'any gay woman.' It's all the others who have the most to lose."

"And the most to fight for."

"Where do you get the right to set them up for a fight they'll lose?"

It was an assault I hadn't planned. I didn't know then how well Joanna Becker had removed herself from the perils of her own convictions.

She looked at me with unflinching calm. "We've always lost. It's not protection you've defined. It's denial. Undoing that is worth getting my ass kicked for."

"What about everybody else's? What about Vicki's?"

"Ask her," she said, and looked at Vicki with an easy possessiveness when she walked out onto the veranda.

Vicki tossed her books and handbag onto the couch. "I certainly object to anyone kicking your ass,"

she said, and leaned over and kissed Joanna,
reaching behind her to take an olive out of a dish
on the table. "What are you two fomenting now?"
She nibbled at the pit and smiled at Joanna. "Have
you restructured the world yet?"

"Toni was telling me how much she agrees with
me," Joanna said.

"Have you? When do the barricades go up?"

We lingered over lunch. I explained that I really
had to get up to the North Shore the next day and
get to work, but that I would continue as advocate
and cautionary advisor. And that I would call on
Aunt Beatrice, to relieve my own unease as much as
anything else.

Vicki threw up a few barricades of her own with
experimental lightness and amiability, opening,
obviously not for the first time with Joanna, the
subject of the projected music workshop tour with
Albertine. Joanna shaved silently at her raspberry
ice, looking directly at Vicki from time to time, a
challenge she countered with the casually occupied
sunny dalliance of an afternoon of butterflies, until
Joanna laughed and said, "I told her once I should
have met her mother first."

"That, Love, would have changed nothing," Vicki
said.

By September, I had sent off twelve of the
scripts I owed Breem. I had my three characters
pretty well in hand, I knew how they behaved and
how they thought. Writing eleven and a half minutes

worth of dialogue for every fifteen-minute episode of their mundane, vacuously comedic lives wasn't very hard to do. That week, Breem had left a message with Valarie: would I call him immediately. Another trip to the grocery up on the highway.

"I'm calling you. What's your trouble?"

"It's a long story."

"Get to the point, this is costing me money."

"You'll get it back. I'm the one who is losing."

"Larry bailed out, right?"

"You guessed it."

"I didn't guess. I know him better than you do. And now you want me to pick up for him. You're right, it will cost you."

"I've got to pay him a kill fee, no matter how lousy his stuff is."

"Show biz. I'll cry with you, but that's all."

"I'll give you his contract plus ten percent for patching up what he did. Plus the rest."

"I may like that; I may not. Send it along. In writing. How do I know his junk can be patched?"

"You can do it, Toni."

"That's not what I'm worried about."

Breem insisted on sending everything directly to me. I told him to send it to the postmaster at Two Harbors and mark it hold. He wanted to know where the hell that was, and I reminded him he didn't need to know; just send it. I thought about selling my soul for the usual mess of pottage, but reflected that even pottage is not that easily come by. I would bend my genius to better things one day. I picked up a loaf of freshly baked bread, six bottles of Fox Head Lager and asked the Swedish lady who ran the grocery and baked the bread every day to slice me some of the ham she had also baked. And I drove back to the cabin.

I stood for a while in front of the wall of windows with my ham sandwich and my glass of beer, watching the gulls circling the wake of a single fishing boat back from a run to check his set lines. Three times, I had called on Beatrice Fröeling. The first time to honor my obligation to introduce myself and to be surprised at how faulty and limiting preconceptions can be. Her being Joanna's great aunt rather than a more immediate, accessible aunt hardly justified the remote, tightly bound, atavistic image of her I had created out of sheer lassitude and simple mental sloppiness. I hadn't put her together with all I knew by then of her militant suffragette background. But I knew I wanted to see her often.

One afternoon not long after that, I had walked up the road from the cabin to the row of mail boxes along the black top highway. The flag was up on Fröeling's box. From the Minneapolis postmark, Joanna's letter had been in there for a few days. At that time, I guess I was deep at work and hadn't felt like going up to the mail box just to find crappy reminders and assorted threats from Breem that I could depend upon Valarie to not monitor, but just relay them up to me. Knowing that, I might not have looked in the box for a week.

Joanna's long letter was filled with conviction, exhilaration, and also with doubts about her revolution. Confessional, almost, in some manifest struggle with her own role in it not too well masked by all the lightly tossed off remarks about Jessi's displeasure. It was filled, too, with an unguarded loneliness, a vulnerability I hadn't expected and didn't especially want to be aware of.

She had, she related, gone ahead with her plans. It seemed fatuous, certainly self-defeating to think of her project as anything but an ad hoc sort of conspiracy. Her probing into the possibility of developing a Women's Law Club sanctioned by the School of Law and the University with the notion of turning it into some sort of hotbed for political action later, seemed to me just plain unrealistic.

She had found this out with her first real encounter with the ruling junta in the School of Law; compellingly in her brush with the Dean of Women. She filled in the details on all this in the letter, along with things like "Jessi threatens to have my head." Jessi's hand did indeed seem heavy on her shoulder. That, I guessed, was what convinced her that her original idea of putting together her off-campus cadre of bona fide women students to storm the battlements later was a more likely weapon. She had the target firmly in her eye. The office of the Dean of Women.

Joanna went after her candidates. One banker's daughter turned out to be a shocked dropout who immediately threatened to report the whole affair to her father. Fortunately, a very real incapacity to grasp the idea added to the difficulty of raising serious alarm in him. The second banker's daughter was another matter. Happy with the whole rebellion idea, she contributed a recruiting job on a young woman undergrad friend who enthusiastically switched majors and filled the gap left by the defector.

Then Joanna added the surgeon's niece and Amy
Larson, the maverick police officer. That made a
committee of five, with Joanna. Plus me, made six.
So she tagged it "Les Six" and left it to everyone
else to figure out who the sixth was. I didn't know
that the name had really come from Vicki who had
borrowed it from an unruly batch of nineteen-
twenties avant garde composers. Joanna had wanted
to add an "e" to the Six, or a "la" or something, but
Vicki's pure French soul, loyal to even an imperfect
androgyny, wouldn't allow it. Joanna bore stoically
this chauvinist male imposition, concentrated on the
revolutionary overtones, and the whole thing became
emphatically "SIX."

SIX conspired and quarreled within itself with
urgent fervor. SIX fomented, SIX spoke out, and
finally SIX marched; tightly, protectively packed
under a SIX banner put together with heady
intemperance by the surgeon's niece. Fortified, rather
to their surprise and Joanna's disapproval, by some
fifty disaffected supporters who mingled a bundle of
uncertain and disparate causes, and with a longing
for success and their original solidarity, SIX occupied
the office of the Dean of Women.

Flanked by her ruthlessly clean and polished
comrades and against a backdrop of all the other
disaffecteds, the encroaching ambiguity of an
unshaven young man with brightly gleaming
dexadrine eyes, and three girls wearing athletic
department sweat shirts, Joanna read her manifesto
with cold determination, an unsparing emphasis on a
new justice for women, and a demand that the
School of Law shape up in particular. Amy,
prudently out of uniform, gave an "Ain't I a law

student?" speech, her mother having made sure Amy put history to effective use.

It's hard to know who was most startled by all this — the Dean of Women, the University, Jessi Ryder, or the newspapers. They were so unaware of any kind of student malaise beyond panty raids or swallowing goldfish that they were obliged to run the story with neither pictures nor a statement from any of the principals save the Dean herself, failing to get any at all from Joanna. After leaving a copy of their demands, SIX had dispersed with a firm hold on their dignity if not a clear idea then of their next move.

Along with her letter, Joanna had sent me the newspaper clippings. I called her from the phone in the grocery.

"Jessi has really asked for my head now. But I'm pretty happy about the whole thing. Although I'm pretty sure I'm going to get thrown out of school. First kick in the ass, right, Branch?"

"I just wish I'd known for sure that Vicki was going to be off workshopping during all this."

"Why?"

"Because it's dumb, her being gone. She shouldn't be. That's why."

"It has nothing to do with you."

"You needn't remind me."

"Albertine had that all planned for months. Vicki wanted to do it. She's doing it."

"And that's all there is to it."

"That's all there is to it."

"So it was Albertine's idea, getting Vicki out of the way."

"You heard what I said."

"Yeah, I heard."

But in this uproar, three people weren't startled. Joanna, who was not going to let the momentum die, despite her proffered misgivings. Vicki, whose graceful and calculated absence was making her own peculiar form of judo rather clear. And Aunt Beatrice. I came to learn that not much startled Aunt Beatrice. Particularly anything about Joanna, or anything Joanna did. Her concerns lay with channeling Joanna's energies, not censuring them.

It is not the quiet of places like the North Shore that we notice. It is the absence of sounds exchanged for the distinct awareness of the movement of water, the rustle of grass. We learn that the breeze has a voice and the cracking of a limb in a tree is as audible an attention to life as the songs of birds and the fussy chatter of the chipmunks in a woodpile. Silence as a different tone of being; something I discovered to be uniquely true about all that surrounded Beatrice Fröeling's house above Duluth. There, perspective was possible.

Stopping the car under the front portico, I turned off the engine and sat in that silence for a few minutes, watching the sunlight move through the piebald birch trees up ahead. A single oak leaf, already turning red from the first frost, fell on the hood of the car. I heard an axe strike wood somewhere beyond the house, hollow and intermittent in the crisp morning air. I pulled the ignition key, made sure Joanna's letter was still in my jacket pocket, and walked around the side of the house looking for Beatrice.

Past the barn, in the orchard, I caught up with her. She was with Carl, deciding the fate, apparently, of the apple trees. As she held my hand briefly, and smiled an otherwise silent hello, I was very aware that she knew why I had come. Carl acknowledged me with a sober nod and moved on to the next tree. With his axe, he struck a blaze in the trunk of each successive tree we passed. The sound of the blows were thick and lifeless in the air, their echo shuddering inside each unresponsive tree.

"Yah, sure. They're all dead, Miss Fröeling." He stood for a moment, the axe hanging heavy in his hand, the faint vapor of his breath pale as his blue eyes against the air.

"Well, it is a pity," she said.

"Wasn't no way to plant, I'll tell you." And he turned hefting the axe again. "Sure thing they was going to go all at once."

"The rest of the orchard was cut off a long time ago, Carl. This is only what is left."

"Yah? Well, I should just cut them down and stack the wood. Get the stumps out before winter. Apple wood is good for the smokehouse."

"Clara will appreciate that."

"Yah, sure." He raised the axe, and struck a branch off the last tree in the row at the foot of the orchard. And shortening his grip on the handle, angled the blade in quick, sharp strokes from left to right, cutting the branch into three short pieces he tucked under his arm.

Beyond the orchard, I could see Joanna's trap

stand surrounded by encroaching brown grass and a swirl of falling leaves. Half a mile away, from the blackness of the thick pine forest, a web of tracks still visible on the frost ran obliquely down to within a few yards of where we stood. Then they circled away to pause in a cluster of wary speculation, and ran off again to double back and disappear down a watchful run along the edge of the forest.

"Damn wolves," Carl said. "Ought to be a bounty on those devils here, too."

"Perhaps, but there isn't going to be on my land," Beatrice said.

"Yah? Well, we'll be the endangered species pretty soon again, I think." And he grinned with a sudden mirthlessness, as though he couldn't quite reconcile his wit with his animosity.

Beatrice put her bare hands into the pockets of her dark mackinaw and glanced at me with a faint smile. "It's the first time she's brought the pack this close. She's still learning to lead."

"She-devil," was Carl's only remark.

"I'd like you to put in new trees in the spring, Carl. So go ahead with the cutting."

And we left him to it and walked back to the house.

The fire in Beatrice Fröeling's sunlit parlor was already blazing up, and I moved away from it to the far end of one of the velvet settees. Beatrice stood for a while in front of the fire, warming her hands while we waited for the coffee she had asked Clara to bring in. Then she laughed and sat down near the fire.

"Joanna always says she thinks I've never gotten

warm since the winter we picketed the White House."

"She told me about that. I wasn't sure I believed it at first."

"Of course we did. There weren't many of us, and it was awfully cold, and mean. Does that surprise you?"

"Not really, I guess. Not that you did it. That it hasn't been done since, what? Nineteen-seventeen?"

"Nineteen-eighteen. But I expect that it will be done again, because it will be necessary."

"And that's what you want Joanna to do?"

Clara brought the coffee steaming in a fat little white pot bordered with a pattern of rose and yellow flowers, and cream and sugar and slices of freshly baked nut cake, arranging it all on the low table between the two settees. Beatrice rose to stir up the fire before she filled our cups. She added a touch of sugar and cream to her own and stirred it slowly for a moment watching the cream swirl and marble on the surface.

"Joanna will do what she feels capable of doing. If that includes remaking the world, as she puts it, I'm sure she will try."

"With the crazy thing she's done? I got her letter today, but I guess there's nothing in it you don't know more about than I do."

"So you came to find out more."

"Yes, I suppose I did. I don't know. I came because I like talking to you. But I'm not sure that talking about remaking the world makes any sense. Or that I want to be part of it anymore."

"There's hardly anything new about

discouragement." Beatrice refilled my cup and I bit
into a piece of the nutcake while she carefully cut a
piece in half for herself. "Except," she added, "seeing
you, or what's more unlikely, Joanna succumb to it."

"She's all fired up now. But those other kids are
just all excited and having fun raising a ruckus.
They'll give up, Beatrice. She'll be left alone with it
then."

"Joanna has often acted alone. To act on
conviction does seem to require an intuitive leap, I
suppose, a faith in knowledge not yet gained."

"Faith and passion are words for fire-eaters. Very
few people survive for long on that diet, I've
discovered."

"I'm sure that's true. Confusing emotion with
conviction is a dangerous thing. People at the head
of mobs always fancy they are leading until they are
run down."

"Or they become tyrants."

"Those are harsh alternatives, both mutually
supporting."

"You really believe there are others? We're not
talking to the point here. I think Joanna's law
school uprising is fueled by all the excitement and
conviction of your rather remarkable past, if you'll
let me put it that way, as it is out of her own.
She's not talking about women law students,
Beatrice. She's talking about all women. Like she
could pick up the whole rights for women and votes
for women, the whole nineteenth century tumult of
anger and ideas and make it happen all over again.
I don't think that can be done."

"There were a great many women before you and
Joanna who were trying to remake the world. They

thought it could be done. And there were many before me who believed the same thing. There will be more."

"Starting over. Again and again. If any of them succeeded, if you did, then why is Joanna out yelling and screaming. Why did I? All of it like talking to the wall."

"I make no claims to success, Ántonia. Only for having taken steps."

"Nobody's got a million years for more steps. What is all this? You're testing me, just like Joanna does."

"My most recent success, certainly."

Maybe it was. Beatrice leaned back in the settee watching me with the same wry, expectant smile that came so easily to Joanna when she was waiting to see where the next thrust was coming from.

"You don't really believe all this, do you," I said. "All the starting over. I know, because Joanna told me. You never did think the vote was the great panacea that would usher in the millennium for women. And you split with those who did. They went home to vote the way they were told. You stayed in the streets to fight for the whole ball of yarn. Yet even you had to fall back. Look, let's just suppose that sometime, I don't know when, we all do pick up on what you did, what Joanna is trying to do. How do we know we won't end up doing what changes nothing and be left to wait for somebody else's daughters to discover how little it mattered? How little we did."

"No, I don't believe in starting over. It really is too late for that. Before Joanna left here, she said something to me. That she just didn't see herself

having written the good word, preached the good
sermon, or marched the good march. Nor sitting in
her mansion waiting for the next generation to
acknowledge her prescience or declare her lack of it.
She's right, Ántonia; you both are. That is why I
think she should fight the School of Law. For
entitlement, if you like, to what she and every
woman equally deserves. But she will learn that
impatience makes angry statements, startles minds,
and leaves events on the same path."

"Minds need startling. They need to be blown
open. For good, not just periodically."

"That, I'm quite sure, is her next step."

Beatrice Fröeling was not one for retracing steps.
She had been a determined, militant, and angry
street fighter for women's rights, one of so many
women who abandoned decorum and gained dignity.
Since the winters of marching and picketing on
Pennsylvania Avenue and the months of argument
and dissension that followed, their numbers dwindled
as they sought to define a future, and she had
quietly withdrawn and banked her fires.

Sheltered within a genteel conspiracy of one, in
that fine old house above Duluth, she had fanned
the coals to flame. She knew she had found herself
all over again in her grand niece, and more. In
Joanna she found the anger that transforms into
persistent, gritty zeal; the excess of passion that
ignites a mind and learns to control itself; the
farsightedness that gathers passionate dreams
together and sets them aright in reality. What she
had taught Joanna was not to re-enlighten the world
on the existence of women's minds, but to know
without equivocation that those minds do exist and

to rely above all on her own. But Beatrice would, very sensibly, leave it to Joanna to learn that pioneers work hard, get hurt, and sorely test their friends. And must make terrible mistakes.

I know that Beatrice Fröeling had, at the outset, some serious reservations about me. Even if, as I also guessed, she knew that Vicki was not the beginning and felt her certainly to not be the end of Joanna's life, she quite decently didn't want things all broken into wild pieces for either of them. Not by anyone. She had made that clear the first time I had called on her. She had done it with a delicate balance of tact and abrupt candor whose meaning was utterly unavoidable, and to ignore it would have been an admission of total lack of the intelligence and taste she endowed me with. Beatrice, like Joanna, is hard to resist.

At that moment, though, I lied just a little. A momentary dalliance aside, I made it clear that I had designs on Joanna of quite a different pattern. I did want to join her revolution. For all my protest, I admit I am easily ignited, and Joanna combusted fires like the wind on a Dakota prairie. With joy and exuberance, burn off old grass for the sake of the new. A state of nature from which I have learned a great deal.

Beatrice walked with me to the door, reminding me to call again. I told her I had to stop in town for some new typewriter ribbon, and had things to finish up and that I would keep in touch. She hesitated, with her hand on the door latch.

"Joanna told me she had gone to South Dakota after pheasant with Jessi Ryder."

"Oh?"

"I'm afraid she was a little unhappy because Jessi was cautioning her about confronting the Dean of Women with a new ultimatum at the start of next semester. Frankly, I think it time for Jessi to be less directive."

"She never mentioned it. Jessi takes her mentor role pretty seriously from what I hear. Maybe she should be told to lay off."

"Perhaps I shall suggest that." Beatrice opened the door for me and as I stepped out, she put her hand on my arm and with a kind of controlled calm she said, "But apparently that didn't bother Joanna nearly as much as Jessi's remarks about Valarie Chase."

"What business is that of Jessi's anyway?"

"None. It's mine now."

"Maybe it is, Beatrice."

I drove the zig-zag of streets down the long hill and stopped at a small stationers and got my ribbon and whatever else it was I needed, and on out Third Street along the lake. A long red ore boat, riding high, coming back for another cargo, moved slowly in under the lift bridge, men on the forward deck lounging at the rail, ignoring the waves of some kids above them on the bridge.

I cut off and picked up the highway that runs along the shore all the way to Grand Portage and the border into Canada. On any bright, clean-washed day like that, the drive back to Joanna's cabin was a charming, relaxed sixty-five miles. Blue spruce and pine grow thick along the road, hemming it in for long stretches. There is a narrow gravel road that cuts into that long, natural green tunnel down to the water where you can drive along a string of stops for tourists to gaze at the lake, marvel at the ever-circling gulls, and climb uneasily down to the water's edge to look for agates among the millions of stones washed round by the waves.

Just beyond Knife River, I stopped at the last rest stop there is on that road to go to the bathroom and eat the hamburger and break open the can of beer I'd bought in Duluth on my way out. I sat on the rocks and looked up the shore as it rose higher and higher above the lake, and thought about Joanna's revolution while I drank my beer.

I thought about the women I knew and how remote the idea of any kind of revolution was from their lives. Women like Carol Reilly whom I'd known for a while in Washington. She was a tall, grey-eyed girl who had enlisted in the army not long after the women's auxiliary had finally been pulled together in the middle of nineteen forty-two. She had served in Italy and in Europe and had ended up as part of the Army of Occupation in the DMZ in Western Germany. The experience changed the world for her.

She came out of it with captain's bars, an enormous ego, and a firm conviction that being a good-looking dyke with a big load of veteran's education benefits was just about the most unassailable thing on earth. She also rode a motorcycle, and was all set to enroll at the University of Southern California School of Medicine. She was going to be a doctor and make a lot of money. And she was going to ride her motorcycle to Los Angeles.

When Carol rode off one morning, her belongings strapped onto her silver Harley Davidson, completing a flourish of calligraphic scrolls in the street in front

of my narrow Washington town house, she became
for me a reminder that innocent assumption, like
virtue, is only its own reward. She had no time at
all for anything except her own personal revolution.
She had no doubts about succeeding, and if she
thought about it all, I guess she was satisfied with
the conventional wisdom. Make your own revolution.
Isn't that enough?

Carol Reilly certainly never saw herself as some
sort of symbol; hers was a personal revolution. If
things are ever to change enough, or move toward
what Joanna Becker imagines, maybe she will. To
justify herself, or to find satisfaction and enjoy a
small touch of scorn for all those newly enlightened.
But at that time, it seemed like everybody was
planning to do something professional and important.
That is, all the gay women I knew had such
ambitions. Or maybe they were conceits.

It was unsettling to challenge such expectations,
to wonder how much of all that would actually turn
into fact. How many of them would achieve such
things. Especially when all the rest of the world was
on a headlong run back into babymaking and
pouring their hearts into the cozy cottage of movie
myth that they were convinced had been dangerously
delayed, if not denied them, by the war. All that
was the only natural dream and desire for any girl.
To reject that, to assume any other place in the
world, was threatening and it was just not natural.
Serving in the army, working in the defense plants
— that was something else. The survival of the
country was at stake. But not then. Only women
who wanted to be men did that. Only lesbians.

I guess that was true enough. Except that none

of the lesbians I knew wanted to be men. For most of them it was a matter of genuine relief that they weren't. For a rare few, it was an absolute celebration. And for one at least it was now a sacred calling.

Joanna Becker had been nurtured with attentive care. All her energies, and the fire in her mind had been set ablaze to lead the revolution. The world is, of course, often troubled by revolutions looking for a leader, but that is a trial not to be compared to the turmoil of soul that ravages a leader looking for a revolution, and draped in the agony of waiting. Joanna had taken the baton from her Great Aunt Beatrice and was already sprinting out on a trackless lap in an unfinished race.

She was creating two things, really. One within herself and another outside for all the others she perceived as like herself. She appeared to have few problems with the internal. With that, she was just naturally on the side of the celebrants. She was determined but, it seemed to me, unclear how to create the freedom and the space to carry the celebration across the whole horizon. To do that, she would have to change the curve of the earth that shaped it. Joanna Becker was, I knew, dangerously ahead of her time.

I dropped my empty beer can inside the paper bag my hamburger came in, watched for a moment as the gulls fought for a piece of bun I had tossed to the rocks below, stuffed the bag in a trash can and drove back to the highway. A big logging truck rolled by, its ground chain bouncing crazily off the blacktop. And suddenly I thought of Valarie.

Beatrice Fröeling would make Valarie her

business for only one reason. Was I imagining things, or was she? Beatrice doesn't imagine things. I don't often lose track of reality while diverted by the heady talk of women taking over the world, but I recovered it fast. Valarie takes over any piece of the world she finds irresistible; she divines vulnerability. Joanna Becker is an irresistible piece. I was not imagining.

At Castle Danger, I pulled in at the little grocery on the highway where my only telephone was. The gravel in front flew against the side of a battered truck, and my own bumper was across the sagging wooden walkway before I stopped. A couple of dirty kids waving licorice whips bolted out of the store and ran across in front of me out into the field in back toward the privies, the screen door banging behind them, the creosote-soaked bundle of cotton hanging on a string from the top bouncing in the air scattering the flies. I grabbed the door before it banged again. Inside at the phone, I took a deep breath and called Valarie.

Across just seven summer weeks, it had been a very flashy affair. Lighting up the velvet night skies around certain parts of Minneapolis with the same sensuous indolence of the weekend fireworks around Lake Calhoun, with the gentle, throbbing penetration of the beat of band music drifting out across the starlit water. Until the skies had darkened and the last lingering rocket had spread out and fallen away, each fiery blossom burning out in a drift of gunpowder smoke and the echo of the exuberant whistle that sent it aloft.

Oh, it was only temporary, of course; just one of those things. Valarie's conspiratorial assurances generally worked soothingly on me with their great appeal to my celebrated adulthood and admirable adjustment. Certainly I could understand compassion for the young, so lonely and confused what with Vicki running off like that, letting Albertine break them up. Joanna, poor baby, needed Valarie's objectivity just then. That's all. Valarie's objectivity simply recognized that it was time for this beautiful, sophisticated kid with the gorgeous body to try out the full range of her talents so she would understand all about distinguishing that from whatever Valarie means by love. How could I object? Joanna wasn't. Valarie did have the advantage there.

I know Valarie, her transparent amusements, her revealing evasions. Yet sometimes I think she is betrayed by some strange, self-truncated maternal uprising, some unconscious nest-building. Snatching at brambles and other deceitfully thorny things in which fledglings find hunkering down in pretty hard going. Especially fledglings like Joanna Becker who've already been winging it with notable success.

But by then, their whole idyll of indulgence, mutual or otherwise as it may have been, had ended in an anti-climactic petulance featuring a new world-weariness Joanna had decided to effect. Or at least that was how Valarie had described it. She may have been right. I would have recognized that had I listened to Vicki with a little more care. She had spent her childhood seeing through the genuine article, and she had grown up both weary of it and able to deflect its influence. Joanna didn't deserve Vicki, and it was just plain unfortunate that Vicki disagreed with that assessment. If now she still did.

It was time to pack my gear. By the next morning, I was ready to roll, but I made one stop first, at Two Harbors for gasoline and to call Beatrice. Up from the boat landing that by then served only fishing boats and an occasional power boat carrying some adventurer from the Wisconsin side across the lake, I parked the car in front of the old three-story Commercial Hotel whose entrance is like a gash cut out of the corner, as though the carpenters who built it in the eighteen-eighties remembered there had to be a way to get in and just hacked it out of the ground floor, leaving the rooms above to hang without support over the walk below.

Inside, the lobby is musty and ill lit, the furniture is upholstered in rusted leather, and a lot of the chairs are rockers with brass spittoons just a sporting chance away. The desk has a higher polish than the bar, and just beyond the lazily revolving pole in front of the barber shop off the lobby are two phones in wooden booths with glass doors frosted halfway up. From a rack in the barber shop, you can buy a Minneapolis paper every day and the *Milwaukee Journal* on Sunday.

I bought a paper and then dialed Beatrice. I told her I had to get back to the city. That it was getting colder and there was snow coming; the paper said so. That I was getting a late start and probably wouldn't make it until some time that night. I told her I had called Valarie and suggested, rather guiltily, that she not worry about Joanna. She remarked that she never worried about Joanna; she just took everything into account. Then I said I would call her again by the end of the week.

That was how I found out that I had passed Joanna sometime that cold, snowy night, somewhere on U.S. 35 on her way to Duluth.

Through The Oriel Window

At seven in the morning, punctual as my habit has long required, I had breakfast on the glassed-in veranda overlooking my back garden. The aging apple orchard was now half cut away, opening the long mile across the forest covering the acres that have been mine to control for more than thirty years. Joanna's trap stand was buried in snow and the tracks of wolves ran distinct, sanctioned and purposefully straight along the edge of the forest.

I set aside the morning paper that lay still folded at my elbow and poured myself a second cup of

coffee. Ántonia's phone call had simply retraced the
path of Joanna's graceless fall into a defensive
self-indulgence as uncharacteristic as it was shabby,
and I considered with some rue the small shock to
my own self-indulgent faith in her. Joanna's
culpability was real enough, but extending its
atonement was a hypocrisy she would certainly reject
and I would not ask for. I sat for some moments
more in that reflective and rather expectant silence,
when quite suddenly it was broken by the sound of
a car, a door slammed shut. Joanna came in through
the kitchen, and I heard her kick off her boots at
the foot of the back stairway in the hall and run up
the stairs and shut her bedroom door.

Clara stood at the entrance to the veranda,
shifting a dish towel from one hand to the other.
"Joanna's come, Miss Fröeling. I knew from the
sound of the car it was her."

"Yes. Would you fix some hot bouillon, Clara, and
some fresh biscuits."

"She looks terribly tired, Miss Fröeling. I think
she drove all night."

"I expect she did." I drew the napkin from my
lap and put it on the table. "Bring the things up to
Joanna's rooms when they are ready, will you,
please."

On my way through the downstairs parlor, I
stopped at my writing desk long enough to open a
drawer and take out a slender key attached to a
piece of black ribbon. Then I went upstairs, passing
through my own rooms into the suite overlooking the
back garden. The draperies in the bedroom were

open and the morning sun was already burnishing the whole expanse of new snow with a brilliant sheen; a release of intense, clear light from within every snowflake.

The room was still in shadow, and the bowl of fresh flowers that was, by my order, placed every morning on the chiffonnier, was reflected back, motionless, caught in the time of the mirror. I touched the petal of one half-open yellow rose and a shower of drops fell from the fresh-washed leaves to the linen doily under the bowl. Chiffonnier: with some amusement, I translated that word into its French — rag-picker.

Quickly unlocking the top center drawer I took from it the familiar worn leather portfolio of letters, tied and bound along its edges with purple braid.

Walking through Joanna's study, I paused for a moment in her small room with the oriel window, watching the sun catch the edges of every furrow the breeze cut on the surface of the lake, and then opened the door to Joanna's bedroom.

I found her exactly where I expected to, lying on her stomach on the bed, her red-stockinged feet hanging over the foot. If she had been asleep, it was reflexive and unknown to her.

"You always know what to expect from me, don't you, Aunt Beatrice."

"That is a comfort I extend to you. And to myself. I dislike surprises, which you know."

Joanna glanced with little apparent concern at the portfolio as I lay it on the clothes press, and then she sat up on the bed watching as I made space on the night stand for the pot of steaming bouillon, one cup, and the biscuits covered with a napkin.

I pulled up the small, cushioned chair. "What time did you leave last night?"

"About ten, I guess. It snowed so hard all the way, it seemed like all night. Maybe it was later than that, I don't know." She turned her wrist to look at her watch. "God, it's after nine o'clock."

She sipped the bouillon and then, between mouthfuls of biscuit she said, "I know you don't. Like being surprised, I mean. That's why you're so calm about it all. This tastes good. Thank you." She gazed intently into the cup, holding it tight in both hands. "Why did I leave. That's what you're really asking." She looked straight at me. "It is, isn't it?"

"It would be pointless for me to tell you why."

"Touché, Aunt Beatrice. But right now you're the only person I would want to tell me."

"What I have always expected is that you be discerning and decisive. And live gracefully with that."

"Living gracefully is a cultural accomplishment. That's not what is difficult. Accepting decisions is."

"There's nothing you lack save greater prescience about some things."

"Taste and judgment. You've told me that before. I'm discovering there are other tastes and other judgments."

"Indeed there are. But it would be regrettable if you were to adopt many of them."

"That is rather isolating, isn't it? Taking on a little rectitude is like walking through a cobweb. It's not easy to see in ordinary light. It sticks and it's hard to get off."

"There are other things equally hard to remove. And as inimical."

"Aren't you being just a little judgmental about my lusts?"

"Not at all. I respect your lusts, as you refer to them. You know that perfectly well. I am suggesting that you do likewise by remembering that they are best bestowed on those who are capable of respect for you."

"Don't sleep with the hired help."

"The hired help are at least honest. Don't sleep with the opportunistic."

"Marvelous. Is anyone else as blessed as I?" Joanna laughed and poured herself another cup of bouillon. She bit into the last biscuit, cupping her hand under her chin to catch the crumbs.

"There have been times when I've questioned honesty's blessedness. The necessity for it is more to the point," I said.

Joanna licked the biscuit crumbs from the palm of her hand. "Its legitimacy at any given moment is the point."

"Exactly. I'll not chide you for an indiscretion I'm sure you've already suffered enough embarrassment from. My concern is for all your other convictions which you appear to have discarded along that path."

"Maybe it was time to re-group. Jessi was pretty adamant about it, anyway. Especially after my little cadre ran off. Everybody ran off."

She set the half empty cup on the night stand

and sat up suddenly, her arms folded across her knees. "Running off is what everybody does. One way or another. Isn't it?"

"They abandon themselves. The rest follows easily enough." Admittedly, my remark was not without calculation, and I waited until I saw Joanna smile in the slow, wry manner I expected.

"Then they realize more than they get credit for," she said. "Those at school — they'll survive their reprimands and lectures from embarrassed parents. Even their suspensions, if they happen, won't mean much. Take off for a few weeks and go to Florida to escape the cold." She leaned back on the pillows again, her hands in front of her, rubbing one thumb against the other. "Except Amy. She's the only one who hasn't run off, and yet she's in the worst trouble. She's been suspended from the police force, and her hearing doesn't come up for three more weeks."

"And she was suspended from the University, as well."

"Of course. Jessi started to say she could take care of that. I told her to lay off. It was a stupid idea that would just make matters worse. I went to Saint Paul and talked to Amy's mother finally about what would happen if Amy got thrown off the force. It wasn't easy, because I know I made all this happen."

"Amy made a choice."

"That choice wasn't there until I made it possible, was it?"

"I can neither sympathize with that nor relieve you of it, Joanna. I can only question it."

"Which means we act alone."

"We do. But never without meaning. That is all that can be shared."

She had pulled off her heavy sweater, her green flannel shirt unbuttoned at the neck. Sitting cross-legged on the bed, she picked up the cup again turning it slowly back and forth in her hands before she spoke.

"You're talking about Vicki, aren't you?"

"You are, Joanna. Only you can."

She said nothing more, just placed the empty cup carefully at her feet.

"I want you to have this now, Joanna," and I lay the portfolio of letters on the bed.

22 Janvier, 1917. Republique Francaise. Place, inconnue ... I return to you this small packet of letters. I do so in sober response to the last request of your dear friend and my comrade in a terrible time. Mademoiselle Fergusson died for the glory of France, for all mankind, and for her own. She was selfless, brave, and her honor will not go unremembered. She rests. May you, and may we all, when this unfortunate war ends. Dans vôtre hônor, je suis, Claudine Lescault, Capitaine; Corps d'Ambulance Cinquant, Croix Rouge.

3 February, 1915. Paris. Beatrice, my dear. ... I think so often of us in our funny little flat in Washington. How hard we worked, how serious and dedicated we were. How much we believed we were at the center of all that mattered. Focus narrows here. The training is arduous, the front is all that is on anyone's arduous, the front is all that is on anyone's mind — and how much longer it will be until we can be of use. I cannot say where we go.... Kiss the cherry blossoms for me when they bloom. Yours always, Gladdis.

18 February, 1915. Washington, D.C. Gladdis, dear ... those two years are now long ago. They will never be, nor will I be nineteen again. 1913–1915. I write them on this sheet of paper and they are in another century. Only the now we are in matters to me ...

October, what date? Dearest.... when we moved forward again. Our unit brought in the wounded from a French cavalry encounter. The animals were crazed as the officers abandon their horses to their agony. I shot one pierced by the stakes the enemy drives into the ground to halt their charge. I can say no more ...

2 December, 1916. Duluth, Minnesota. Gladdis, my dearest. I cannot know if any of my letters to you are censored by the authorities. It matters little now, it seems to me. Surely the horrors of all these days far overshadow any pain my feelings for you can ever inflict upon the world should it be obliged to make them a concern. I rely on your wisdom and keenness of mind, and I try to content myself with that. But my agnostic soul cannot refrain from offering a prayer for your safety all the while. Somehow, if my arms could shelter you, if I could put my love together with yours once again, you would be safe now and we would then both be so. Should you leave the sector, advise me in the manner we agreed upon. I follow the dispatches in the paper daily. I will know where you are ...

23 December, 1916. Dearest Beatrice, ... in haste, everything intensifies. The bombardment does not cease. We leave ***** by the ***** road to move back to the village of ***** where we will be operating at the trenches seven kilometres in advance of the first field dressing station for as long as possible. This line cannot hold. God has forsaken us, not we him ...

My Dear Victoria — I need not tell you that Joanna has been with me these past weeks — exhausting herself with long, pointless hikes in the snow and cold, pacing about the house and staring out the windows, looking, I assume, for you and what she ought to restore. Rather than see her continue to gnaw away at this knot of remorse, expecting to elicit from me sympathy and direction I am not at all sure she would make the desired use of, I have suggested that she respect your intelligence and balance, however much she exhibits so little of her own. I believe you are the only fixed point in her life now.

It was once suggested to me that Joanna

didn't deserve you. That she is now struggling with the unsettling idea that she owes you her gratitude for the privilege is an advantage I rely on you to advise her of. I hope all you hold dear in her will allow that.

With great affection — Beatrice

I stood in the middle of our bedroom and read Beatrice Fröeling's letter to me over again. I had returned to the house on Lake Of The Isles and for the past eight nights had slept alone in that room. And I knew, even before it was sanctioned again by the appealing candor that had granted so much in the past, I no longer wanted to.

"Vicki —" The flat edge of caution in Joanna's voice didn't quite mask her doubt.

"I called because I need to talk to you, Joanna. I'll be at the cabin at Split Rock. As soon as I can get there. Tomorrow."

The whole silent drive was a deliberate fog in my mind except for the stretch beyond Duluth. By then, I could grant the existence of the lake, the nature of the evening, and the traffic of occasional cars and logging trucks that passed in the opposite direction. I was aware of the blacktop, wet and still gleaming under the glare of headlights; of one of those last, brief, false thaws that promise spring will somehow follow after winter finally locks the land. And aware that Joanna, in my mind, was fixed in form and yet untethered, as illusory as the infinite point of the road ahead.

Beyond Castle Danger, past the row of mail boxes on nine posts at Split Rock, I turned off the highway, down the narrow road to the cabin, a little surprised to be following a shadowed trail of double tracks in the snow. Joanna had left the garage door up. I drove in beside her car, and annoyed myself with some foolish guilt at having put my bare hand on the hood to find it quite cold.

Joanna had been there well ahead of me. She had brushed the snow aside and gathered an armload of firewood from the neat pyramid stacked beside the cabin. The heat from the butane vent shivered against the evening sky, and the smoke from the fireplace rose straight up. I was getting distressingly cold, my hands and feet a little numb as I chose a careful way past her footprints that had crushed the snow down into the layers of brown pine needles. I reached the steps without looking up until I realized that Joanna had opened the door at the top, and was standing against the light, waiting for me.

For the first time, I felt that I was in danger of wearing hurt like an aggressive tarnish, that my voice would betray a risk I knew was false. That I would hazard a game neither of us needed to play.

"You look half frozen. Come in."

"I'm glad you noticed, because I am."

The sweep of the lighthouse beam repeated its arc from the breadth to the length of the lake, startled the Wisconsin shore, and then spent itself down the long, black distance toward Michigan. From the chair by the fire I gazed through the long row of windows up the shore at the high rock point where the lighthouse stood dark in that moment against the black lake.

"I never realized that that light was so clear. It transforms space. Like seeing the moon as a hole in the sky."

"Sometimes cutting holes in the night is a very necessary thing," Joanna said.

"Out there, too. No?"

Joanna sipped at the last of her drink apparently deciding to let that one go. "The lighthouse was a sort of afterthought," she said. "A compensation for oversight. There used to be a passenger boat called The Castle, one of those that ran the lakes from Duluth through Sault Sainte Marie and back again in the nineteen-hundreds. It ran aground one night on the sand bar down there at Castle Danger in one of those terrible storms that only the Norwegian fishermen seem to know how to ride out."

"That's a lovely name for so awful a place."

"A few people were saved. By the fishermen and their wives and daughters. The old women still talk about it because they were the daughters. And their daughters mix stories they heard as children with the scrapbooks their grandmothers kept and the big double-spread picture of the wreck from the Sunday brown pages that hangs framed in the dining room of a house down the shore."

Joanna was silent for a moment, and then she picked up my empty glass and went into the kitchen. The dinner she had prepared seemed a surprising bit of contrition. Joanna had never before made anything but a pot of coffee, that I could remember. She laughed about it, said that Clara had really fixed it and told her to keep it properly warm in the butane oven.

We ate in front of the fire, sitting on a couple of cushions from the couch, at the long pine coffee table. She poured a little wine into my glass, waiting for my appraisal with just the hint of her familiar smile. Whether it was a defensive tactic or a simple need to talk of things meant to reveal what I chose to see, I left to chance.

"I ate dinner often in that room because that was Clara's family home," she said. "Before my mother died, it seemed like visiting my Aunt Beatrice meant being looked at in the same searching way I knew the lighthouse revealed the shore. I was being found out. Clara's house was a safer place. And Carl, too. He knew things even my father was ignorant of. Like how to build a fire right, anywhere. And how to read the track of the wolves in the snow and what the look in the eye of the leader meant, watching you out of the angle of a lope-footed stride, leading the pack away."

She leaned over the fire and pushed at a half-burned log with the poker, rolling it to the back until a shower of sparks drifted up, watching the flame until it settled into a steady, bright burn.

"My father," she said quietly, "is an odd thing to be talking about."

"Why is it odd? Thinking about fathers."

"Because I have always thought I sorted that out a long time ago."

"So had I."

"And you haven't?"

"I don't really know — or even that it matters. Sometimes I traveled with him on concert tours when he wanted me to, without wanting to do it; all over Europe, attaching myself to countries and cities and streets and bridges and all sorts of things in an effort to save the self I was with my mother. We would stay with his friends or patrons usually in big houses where I could keep some kind of space between us. But sometimes we would have to stay in small hotels. Always in one room, because there wasn't money for privacy. And I would try to get up first to be out of the way, as though his rehearsal was more important than my need to get out of that room to just walk on the streets by myself."

Joanna was listening with a grave detachment I had not quite seen in her before. As if, through this odd recital she had moved away from herself enough to risk knowing me in a way beyond her control. I divided the rest of the bottle of wine between us. Warmed by the fire, its bouquet had heightened and I knew exactly why I had come back to Joanna.

"So you won't have to ask again, I'll finish this story. One night, during a concert in Milan, I sat there watching the orchestra just like I'd done hundreds of times before, and I suddenly realized that my father looked just like all the rest of the violins. Just like all the rest of the orchestra. A human shape in a black tuxedo, a shirt front white as tile, his face lost in light. The next day we were scheduled to go on to Rome. I went back to Paris alone. I went back to my mother. To my mother and my mother's friends, and to my own. To women, I guess you would say."

"And that's why you're here now."

"I'm here because I'm still in love with you. More than I thought I could be."

"And because it's time, at last, to stop running back to Albertine."

"Joanna, I didn't run to my mother. Where I went doesn't matter. I went back to our house — without you.

"And I ran for shelter to Aunt Beatrice. I know." Joanna stared hard into the fire and shook her head in her own disbelief.

"Aunt Beatrice — Mother, they'll always be a part of us. All of them will be. Even Valarie."

"I'm not asking you to forgive me that."

"I don't. The world is full of Valaries. It wasn't you Valarie wanted. It was herself."

"It's hardly Valarie you have to validate."

"Would you rather it was you?"

"No."

"That's right. You will validate yourself. And that will be all that's necessary. Your Aunt Beatrice told me that once when I wasn't listening."

"Aunt Beatrice's approval is often inseparable from her idea of good manners. What one does seldom risks censure, only how one chooses to do it."

"It's just possible we all would be better off with ideas for parents, for families," I said.

"Parents are ideas," Joanna laughed. "And so are families. My Great Aunt Beatrice is the only grandmother I ever had. As though there was always something between us that transcended what is traditional to receive. She's really given me what I needed most. What I thought I could have only by hazarding the outrage of a great many people, and the honesty of a few. Her candor has clarified a lot of things for me. Maybe she's been my only mother, too."

"Then our mothers fail us, too," I said. "They leave us at risk to find for ourselves where we belong."

"That's saying their mothers failed them. But there seems to be something else going on. Or not going on. Why did Aunt Beatrice and all of them simply re-learn and repeat what women living in decades remote from them learned and said? As though those women were talking into the wind and it blew back and disappeared. They talked only to themselves and the wind and what they said died into silence.

"I spent almost two years in Aunt Beatrice's library reading books I never found anywhere else, that talked about things I'd never heard anywhere except in my own head. A lot of time reading about light and that kind of darkness."

Joanna began to pick up the dishes and take them into the kitchen. She came back opening a fresh pack of cigarettes, and lit one for me from a coal in the fire. "Don't get up, Vicki. We're out of wood. Just look at this for me. I'll be back in a few minutes." On her way out, she pulled a windbreaker from a hook beside the door and I heard her go down the steps.

That was when I saw her Aunt Beatrice's correspondence with Gladdis Fergusson for the first time.

* * * * *

Joanna was standing in the doorway, a trace of snow across her shoulders and in her hair, some firewood in a canvas carrier, more under one arm. "It's still snowing pretty hard. I don't think you'll be driving back to Duluth tonight. If that's what you intended."

"I hadn't."

"No." And she shook up the fire, adding fresh logs, stacking the rest of them beside the fireplace. She was turned away from me, all her attention on coaxing the fire. "Don't ask me about it, Vicki. Not yet."

Never had I seen Joanna so tightly controlling tears she had revealed only to the firelight. If she was aware of the ambiguity in her remark, or the complexity in her brief, intense struggle, I had no need to ask. She had told me.

I closed the folder with Beatrice's letters inside, and tied it with the purple braid. Joanna had lit a cigarette and sat on the floor, leaning against the couch.

"Did you know this?" I asked.

"Yes. I knew about it. But never what happened to them. Does it surprise you?"

"Not when I thought about it, no. About the rooms upstairs, the flowers. A lot of things — the picture of Gladdis. Do you know how it happened?"

"Aunt Beatrice wasn't able to find out until almost a year later. You remember your history. In December of nineteen-sixteen, the German army broke through the French lines and drove for Paris. The dressing station and the field hospital were abandoned. The ambulances with the wounded attempted to flee with the rest."

"She was buried in France?"

"Yes." Joanna threw her cigarette into the fire.
"Vicki, going to Duluth to see my Aunt Beatrice
became a kind of game for me by the time I was
twelve or thirteen — a game of getting away from
afternoon tea. My mother would ask for coffee
instead and fill her cup half way with brandy. That
was the moment for getting away. I would go
through the back hall, upstairs to those rooms. They
filled me with fear and a terrible, bristling need to
discover who it was that seemed to know me in
there. Who spoke to me with a voice beyond sound,
that I could answer without speaking. The silence
told me more every summer's visit, until all the
disconnected stories, all the guarded, half-completed
phrases, all the puzzling disarray of a past time
when Aunt Beatrice and Gladdis joined with those
who meant to move the world, fell into place.

"One summer afternoon, after I'd been reading by
myself, in the window seat in the oriel window, I
stopped on the way downstairs to tea, in the
doorway of that suite, and I remember looking at
the flowers on the chiffonnier, reflected in the
mirror, and beside them at the picture of Gladdis.
That was when I guessed the rest."

Leaning against a pillow at the arm of the couch,
I stretched my legs out, my stockinged feet just
touching Joanna's shoulder as she sat on the floor
facing the fire. The wind had turned, coming down
the lake dashing snow against the long, black row of
windows. The light from Split Rock would diffuse
and lose itself in the snow or suddenly reappear
whenever the errant wind would swirl the night
clear.

"Vicki, why did she wait so long to give me those letters? To make it easier for me to say I've known for so long that those rooms were for Gladdis? Maybe it was easier for her. But it shouldn't have been that way for them, even if they thought it had to be. We made our place, she told me. What kind of place was denial while they hid in each other and tried to change the whole world to make their own place in it? Because the world would not change for us, she told me.

"If Gladdis hadn't been killed, what then? Things would have been quite different, she said. We would have gone on to make a greater place. As you will. Aunt Beatrice has made my place so far, Vicki. I've been hearing her story for so long, reading her books, getting angry through her anger. The anger is right. She saw it all, she and Gladdis, and all those others."

In the silence, I listened to the snow tapping against the windows, the hesitant whisper of the fire when the wind would sweep across the chimney-opening outside. Joanna got to her feet, looking down at me for a moment, and unfolded the knit afghan on the back of the couch and put it across my legs.

All those others — Joanna had been led back into the fire of their time. Her attraction to their anger, to their passionate vision, and the despair she shared at its final blurring had left her at the farthest edge of certitude. All those women, tight-waisted, in long, difficult skirts, marching and carrying signs, wide ribbons of protest and proclamation across their breasts. I don't suppose any of them were just like that, in the old newsreels. It's necessary to slow them down. They must have used those gestures, peculiar to their time, fitful and unlikely. But the tempo is history. Aunt Beatrice and the others on the sidewalk outside that black iron fence at the White House, their vigil fire in a trash can, the flames whipping out like paper streamers in the wind. Suffragettes in black and white moving in jagged purpose and anxiety, sixty broken frames a minute. What is lost, is what informed them; they were consumed in ways those pictures don't reveal. There is no way to judge them by that, nor let what will come next be reduced to jerks and empty pauses, and disconnected leaps.

Joanna came back from the kitchen with two brandies and sat down on the couch beside me. And smiled at last in her familiar, odd way. "Once when I was about seven, I guess, I read something about sculpture and the lost wax method. Because it was never explained in that book, just referred to, I figured it meant some sort of great loss to art and the whole development of sculpture, and while it seemed sad and unfortunate, I wondered how things that important just got lost as if somebody wrote that procedure on a piece of paper and it got tossed out with a heap of fifteenth century trash.

"I guess it was that problem — how and why things get lost, that made me look far enough until I found out the whole thing was about molds and casting and melting away. Or about who wants things lost.

"Sometimes I feel like I'm standing behind some enormous plate glass that stretches beyond me in all directions, and I'm yelling about all this that I know and no one hears or listens. There are a lot of loss makers out there.

"And I don't want to handle any more loss for a while, Vicki."

A few of the publications of
THE NAIAD PRESS, INC.
P.O. Box 10543 • Tallahassee, Florida 32302
Phone (904) 539-5965
Mail orders welcome. Please include 15% postage.

A CERTAIN DISCONTENT by Cleve Boutell. 240 pp. A unique
coterie of women.   ISBN 1-56280-009-4 $9.95

GRASSY FLATS by Penny Hayes. 256 pp. Lesbian romance in
the '30s.   ISBN 1-56280-010-8   9.95

A SINGULAR SPY by Amanda K. Williams. 192 pp. 3rd spy novel
featuring Lesbian agent Madison McGuire.   ISBN 1-56280-008-6   8.95

THE END OF APRIL by Penny Sumner. 240 pp. A Victoria Cross
Mystery. First in a series.   ISBN 1-56280-007-8   8.95

A FLIGHT OF ANGELS by Sarah Aldridge. 240 pp. Romance set at
the National Gallery of Art   ISBN 1-56280-001-9   9.95

HOUSTON TOWN by Deborah Powell. 208 pp. A Hollis Carpenter
mystery. Second in a series.   ISBN 1-56280-006-X   8.95

KISS AND TELL by Robbi Sommers. 192 pp. Scorching stories by
the author of *Pleasures*.   ISBN 1-56280-005-1   8.95

STILL WATERS by Pat Welch. 208 pp. Second in the Helen
Black mystery series.   ISBN 0-941483-97-5   8.95

MURDER IS GERMANE by Karen Saum. 224 pp. The 2nd
Brigid Donovan mystery.   ISBN 0-941483-98-3   8.95

TO LOVE AGAIN by Evelyn Kennedy. 208 pp. Wildly
romantic love story.   ISBN 0-941483-85-1   9.95

IN THE GAME by Nikki Baker. 192 pp. A Virginia Kelly
mystery. First in a series.   ISBN 01-56280-004-3   8.95

AVALON by Mary Jane Jones. 256 pp. A Lesbian Arthurian
romance.   ISBN 0-941483-96-7   9.95

STRANDED by Camarin Grae. 320 pp. Entertaining, riveting
adventure.   ISBN 0-941483-99-1   9.95

THE DAUGHTERS OF ARTEMIS by Lauren Wright Douglas.
240 pp. Third Caitlin Reece mystery.   ISBN 0-941483-95-9   8.95

These are just a few of the many Naiad Press titles — we are the oldest and
largest lesbian/feminist publishing company in the world. Please request a
complete catalog. We offer personal service; we encourage and welcome direct
mail orders from individuals who have limited access to bookstores carrying
our publications.